DEPTHS OF DECEIT

KELLIE WALLACE

SOUL MATE PUBLISHING

New York

DEPTHS OF DECEIT

Copyright©2018

KELLIE WALLACE

Cover Design by Ramona Lockwood

This book is a work of fiction. The names, characters, places, and incidents are the products of the author's imagination or are used fictitiously. Any resemblance to actual events, business establishments, locales, or persons, living or dead, is entirely coincidental.

Published in the United States of America by
Soul Mate Publishing
P.O. Box 24
Macedon, New York, 14502

ISBN: 978-1-68291-703-9

ebook ISBN: 978-1-68291-681-0

www.SoulMatePublishing.com

The publisher does not have any control over and does not assume any responsibility for author or third-party websites or their content.

For my son.

(Do not read this book until you're old enough!)

Acknowledgments

Thank you to my beta readers who made this book so much better. To my family for their support and to my readers. Without you, I wouldn't be here.

Chapter 1

Elias Dorne sipped his chilli cream iced coffee and curled his lip with a grimace. The coffee might've been tasteless, but the view of Sydney's Harbour Bridge glistening through the steel buildings made up for it. "Is this what I trekked six blocks for?" he exclaimed. "A stupid social media fad?"

"Oh, quit your whining," Daisy Henderson quipped, her slim lips pulling into a smirk. Best friends since high school, Elias thought they were on the brink of a romance, but it had never quite happened, stagnant and idle. Daisy nudged him forcefully. "Hand it over. You dragged me out on my lunch break to stand in line with other millennials. You owe me a taste."

"I'm pretty good at ignoring promotional posts on my feed," Elias remarked, watching a group of young women taking selfies with their chilli cream coffees. "But Soho Café's posts sucked me right in."

"That's the power of social media. A good PR company targets people like you—hardened, ignorant, difficult to persuade. You ridicule the power of social media and look where it got you."

"Just drink the damn coffee." Elias studied Daisy as she drained the cold drink, searching for disgust or doubt on her face. She clicked her tongue when she was done and handed the cup back.

"You're right. It's just water with a splash of chilli powder and coffee flavouring." Daisy hooked her handbag over her shoulder. "The café opened last week. I heard it's owned by a couple of hippies, so they probably hired a PR company to help with the opening. I feel sorry for them. This social media experiment has failed big time."

"They won't last one week in this city," Elias replied with disappointment, tossing his beverage into a nearby bin. "People around here like their coffees hot, large, and exciting."

"Sounds like what most women want in a man," Daisy said with a laugh.

They coursed their way through the streets of Sydney CBD, curling their collars against the brief, crisp wind sweeping between the skyscrapers. Men and women in business attire marched by, mobile phones attached to their ears, enveloped by the loud city ambience—honking horns, singing buskers, and music spilling out from fashion outlets.

"Have you put your resignation in yet?" Daisy asked as they reached the pedestrians' corner.

"I haven't had the balls to write it up yet," Elias replied. "Everyone's been putting their notices in. Every time I want to do the same, I'm guilt-ridden for abandoning the studio."

Elias's role as production manager for Manny Magpie TV, a local television studio, seemed glamorous at first, but five years later, it was becoming mundane, repetitive, and exhausting. He wanted out, a chance to start something new and fresh.

"That may be so, but think of the long hours and the stress you've been under," Daisy argued. "You have a generous wage, but so what? Besides, it's not your fault your boss hired a closeted drug addict. He should've done a background check or been on set when Adam went berserk on TV. What was Adam hyped up on again?"

"Ice, I think."

"Did he lose his job?"

"Hell yeah. He was thrown in jail and Bill lost his credibility. The police shut the whole station shut down for a week. It was unbelievable."

"The studio's owned by that rich magnate, isn't it? Everything's on show these days, Elias. Appearances are everything."

They joined the crowd crossing the street. The sun beamed down from above, promising a warm summer's day. The city had numerous pockets where it would feel like summer and winter in one season. Elias could already feel beads of sweat rolling down his back. He manoeuvred through the pulsating sea of business people and paused outside an electronics store and stripped his jacket, hooking it over his arm. Daisy was dressed in a floral print skirt and apple-green top, her red heels accentuating the tight curves of her calves.

The wind picked up, playing with the hem of her skirt, giving Elias a snippet of a lace petticoat. "I heard Blue Tail Media is looking for staff," Daisy advised, slipping her arm through his when they rejoined the crowd. "The new owner is trying her hardest to rebuild the company after the scandal."

"Is this the same company with the CEO and his wandering penis?"

Daisy smirked at him. "The very one. I doubt Bobbie Hayes expected it to go as public—and as scandalous—as it did. Don't you think it was strange the CEO resigned quietly *before* his former secretary Lily Harolds came out alleging that he sired her four-year-old son? I know a woman at the gym who's friendly with Lily. Apparently she was a virgin when he bedded her."

Elias groaned. "It's all hearsay."

"I doubt it. Hayes was known for his wandering eyes, despite being married to law attorney, Justine Banks. She was adamant her husband was a victim in Lily's web of lies."

Elias recalled seeing the attorney's slim, pale face plastered across the news defending her husband's accusations. "Isn't it a bit coincidental that no one else has come forward slandering Hayes?"

Daisy's lips pursed together. "I think there's more girls out there. Maybe Hayes's wife is paying for their silence. I guess we'll never know."

They walked past a bus shelter emblazoned with pretty pink advertisements designed for women: makeup, sanitary products and perfume. "Blue Tail Media publish women's interest magazines, don't they?" Elias asked.

They stopped outside a news agency and Daisy escorted him to the rows of fashion magazines at the front of the store. She picked up one entitled *Bella* and flicked through it. "This is the September issue. Look, I can show you what Ava publishes—"

Elias snapped the magazine from her fingers and sorted through the pages with a raised eyebrow. "Look at these fucking headlines: 'How to get your crush to like you.' 'Dominate your man in the bedroom.' 'Win your ideal job.'" He slid the magazine back on the rack. "You expect me to write this drivel? I have a Bachelor of Arts in Media and Communication. I'm not giving up five years of university to write for horny housewives."

Daisy threw her hands up in the air. "You know what? It's fine. I'm just trying to help you," she said, batting his hand away when he reached for her. "You want out of your current job and Ava Wolfe needs someone with experience. It may be a win/win situation. I'm friends with the editor of *Bella* so I can probably set up an interview for you."

Elias exhaled a breath and ran a hand through his short, black hair. He'd heard of Ava Wolfe's questionable reputation over the years, the tyrant in the red dress. She was ruthless in the boardroom and unkind to her interns, acquiring a new worker every four months.

From the age of twenty-three, Ava had built her empire from nothing, purchasing dying media companies to resurrect them for a profit. She would definitely be a challenging and formidable boss to work for. Was he ready for the demands of Ava Wolfe?

"So what is it, Elias?" Daisy pressed, tilting her head to the side, her blue gaze piercing. "The window's closing. Do you want a new job or not?"

It was now or never. "All right, please set up the interview. Text me the day and time when you hear back."

Daisy poked him in the ribs. "Hey, you could at least say thank you, you ungrateful bastard."

"Sorry, I've got a lot on my mind. You know how much I appreciate you doing this."

She flashed him a wide grin. "I know. I complete you."

When Elias returned to the office, he started working on his resignation letter.

~ ~ ~

At seven o'clock, Elias walked in the door and dumped his briefcase and mobile phone on the kitchen bench. Bone-weary and tired, he switched on the television in time for the news and buried his head in the refrigerator, looking for something to eat.

After making a ham and cheese sandwich, he flopped onto the couch, bringing with him a handful of magazines published by Blue Tail Media. He felt a little foolish paying for them at the supermarket, lying to the checkout girl that they were for his girlfriend.

Taking a bite of his sandwich, Elias searched through the pile for *Bella* and flipped through the articles, getting a grasp on the writing style and format. If Daisy got him an interview, he had to be prepared.

As he added *Bella* to his reading pile, he picked out a gossip magazine. His motives weren't entirely innocent. Elias had hoped to see something in there about Ava. Maybe the paps caught her doing the walk of shame or attending an event with a mysterious man. It was worth a shot. He scanned through it hastily as if worried he would get caught. Flashy images of famous movie stars and television personalities stared back at him.

The rhythmic buzzing of his mobile phone sounded from the kitchen and he bounced off the couch to answer it.

"What's the news, Daisy?"

"Are you free on Friday at two p.m.?"

"I can shuffle my schedule around." Excitement and anxiety coupled in Elias's gut. He had no idea what to expect. The future of Blue Tail Media was still up in the air. Was he prepared to go down with the ship if everything failed? "Did you speak to the editor or Ava specifically?"

"I spoke with the editor Blake Parker," Daisy replied. "In fact, there's been a change in plans. They filled the copywriter position a few weeks ago, but a new role has become available." She paused. "Unofficially, Ava's been looking for someone to manage all business communications and marketing. Her previous secretary couldn't keep up with her crazy demands and workload. Blake said he's happy to interview you if you're still interested. He was impressed by your résumé."

"Of course. What's the job?"

"It's pretty big, Elias. She's looking for a Director of Communications. How cool is that? You'll be in charge of all press releases, articles, public relations and communication for Blue Tail Media. In lieu of the bad press, Ava wants an expert in damage control to change the company's public image. It won't be easy, but you're more than qualified."

"I can do that. What else is there?"

"The usual ad-hoc tasks. Blake mentioned the candidate must be prepared to accompany Ava on business trips."

"So, basically be her glorified assistant?" Elias said.

"Director of Communications," Daisy corrected. "This is a massive role. There's a lot more responsibility here than the TV studio. Look Elias, if you don't want to attend the interview—"

"What's the pay like?"

"Blake wouldn't tell me. He said it's up to you and Ava to discuss."

Elias rapped his fingers on the kitchen bench. The notion of sitting behind a desk all day, pumping out articles to appease the public didn't appeal to him. However, the job—if he got it—would open up massive doors later on. *Elias Dorne, Director of Communications* had a nice ring to it. If he could tolerate working with Ava Wolfe for twelve to eighteen months, then he could do anything.

"All right, I'll see Blake on Friday. Good night, Daisy."

Chapter 2

On the morning of the interview, Elias woke at five a.m., went for a run in the park, showered, and caught the early train into work. When he stepped onto the fifth floor, the office was empty, washed in a pale white glow from the fluorescent lights. He heard the reverberating growl of the cleaner's vacuum in the board rooms.

After making a coffee, he sat down at his desk and spent the next hour reading up on Blue Tail Media and Ava Wolfe. He searched Facebook, social media accounts, and news sites for any background information on the CEO. He dug up enough information to form an understanding of the infamous Ava Wolfe.

At thirty-four, Ava was divorced, had no children, and was known in quiet circles for her "promiscuous" reputation. According to some, she had a revolving door of men at her beckon call. She was often featured in trash magazines sneaking out of a lover's house.

Elias considered himself relatively handsome, with his lean, athletic frame, ink-black hair, and clear blue eyes, but he wasn't a womaniser, only ever having slept with two women in his life.

It was clear from the crap the tabloids were printing that Ava loved men, loved being around them, and being in bed with them. Would he be able to resist her? Could she resist him?

The first wave of employees trickled into the office at eight o'clock, followed by a morose-looking Bill Gander, dressed in a crumpled shirt and over-washed pair of jeans.

Not wanting a confrontation regarding his resignation letter, Elias slipped from his desk and went down to the studio. He hung in the shadows, silently working until it was time to leave.

Blue Tail Media was located three stations away from Manny Magpie TV, based in Lido Place, a pedestrian-only plaza accommodating luxury stores, banks, television networks, and a post office.

Elias wandered the sun-drenched mall, his portfolio banging against his leg, spending some time to relax before his big interview. Grabbing a quick takeaway coffee, he crossed the plaza, stopping outside a ten-storey, stone building eclipsing the afternoon sun. The gold lettering on the glass doors read *Blue Tail Media.*

Elias drew a calming breath and entered the lobby. The blonde receptionist sitting behind the curved marble desk gazed up from typing and smiled.

"Good afternoon."

Elias approached the desk. "Hello, I'm Elias Dorne. I'm here to see Blake Parker at two o'clock."

"Sure, please sign in on the ledger in front of you and I'll call for Blake."

To kill some time, Elias watched people enter the lobby as the elevator doors opened and studied every woman that emerged, wondering if Ava Wolfe may be among them. He'd seen her picture in editorials and on the news, but never in person.

"Mr. Dorne," the receptionist called him back over. "I'm afraid Blake's been called into an urgent meeting, so Ms. Wolfe will see you instead." She jerked her chin towards the lifts. "Please ride up to level four and Ms. Wolfe's office is on the right."

Elias thanked her, gathered his things, and hopped into the elevator. When he stepped out, he was greeted by two glass doors sealed with a security lock. If he turned his head, he could see a camera pointing at him in the corner of the ceiling. *Heavy artillery.*

He pressed a buzzer on the door and waited to be let in. The office was open planned, clean, and bright, with a grand view of the Sydney Harbour Bridge piercing the sky. A staff member directed him to the boardroom and instructed him to wait for Ava.

Elias sat at the table, tapping his foot methodically, getting more nervous by the minute. Keeping his hands busy, he opened his writing portfolio and spread out his best pieces across the desk. Hopefully, his work would impress the boss.

As if on cue, the door opened, and Ava Wolfe entered the room, carrying a notepad, a coffee cup, and his résumé. "Thank you for meeting me, Mr. Dorne."

Elias swivelled in his seat and his body immediately betrayed him. Blood rushed below his belt at the sight of her, causing him to stay pinned to his chair as she stuck out her hand. Crowned with a headful of springy, copper curls, Ava was dressed in a royal-blue, knee-length dress, accentuating her wide hips and petite waist. A pearl necklace disappeared into the chasm between her breasts.

When she sat down opposite him, Elias understood why this woman had a cohort of rumoured lovers. Ava was breathtaking. She was blessed with wide, green eyes, a slim nose, and lush, plump lips splashed in red lipstick, the perfect hue to match the fieriness of her hair.

"Thank—" Elias cleared his throat, having difficulty finding his tongue. "Thank you for giving me this opportunity."

"I promise I won't take up too much of your time, Elias." Lowering her gaze to his résumé, Ava tilted her head to one side. "You're currently employed at Manny Magpie TV. Is that correct?"

"Yes, ma'am."

"What does your role involve?"

"I'm the production manager, so I assist in the studio, setting up the cameras, script work, corresponding with the performers, editing, and post production."

"Do you write copy?"

Elias referred to his portfolio spread out across the table. "All my y freelance and contracted work is in here including pieces I've written for Manny Magpie."

Ava's gaze flicked upward. "The studio was involved in a scandal recently. An actor high on ice went berserk on live television. I saw it on the news."

Elias bit the inside of his cheek. "Yes, that's right. The company has since moved on from the incident."

"Did you have any part in damage control? I can imagine something like that would deeply affect the public's influence."

He nodded in agreement. "Yes, my main concern was minimising the negative perception caused by the airing. As soon as the situation came to my knowledge, I published a blog explaining the mistake the studio made, followed by an apologetic email to our advertisers. You'll find in my portfolio a public apology I released with the assistance of a PR company."

"What were the results of your work?"

"They were generally positive. Our ratings were still down and stakeholders believed going off the air would be beneficial. However, I fought for the decision to stay on. I surmised that in going off the air the studio would be accepting defeat."

"I agree. Did you work on your own or had a team around you?"

"I worked solely by myself. The studio manager entrusted me with managing all public relations and communications."

"So, you were second-in-command?"

"Yes, I guess so."

"I want to be honest with you, Elias." Ava leaned back in her chair and crossed one leg over the other, giving him a momentary flash of milk-white skin. "I'm sure you've heard the rumours regarding this company's previous management. As you can imagine, right now I'm in damage control. I need the help of someone who can alter the public's perception of this company. Contain the damage. You'll be amazed how long the stink of a scandal can linger, even when the company has been bought out. Nothing is worse than the Australian media. They will chew you up and spit you out." She tapped his CV with a manicured fingernail. "You're more than qualified for the position and Blake was very adamant in pushing your application forward." Her emerald gaze penetrated his soul. "I remind you the role of Director of Communications is not for the faint of heart. It involves long hours and you'll be on call twenty-four/seven. If I need something, I'll make contact, no matter what time of day or night." She pursed her lips together and gave him a cursory look over, a glance that made him uncomfortable. "Are you married? Do you have a family?"

Thinking it was an odd thing to ask, Elias shook his head. "No, I'm single."

"Elias, I'm not like other employers. I take serious interest in my staff's wellbeing and I try to create a good work-life balance here. If you'd told me you had young children, I probably would've denied your application on the spot. This company is everything to me, Elias. I need someone to be one hundred percent committed." A small smile peaked her lips. "Are you still interested in pursuing your application?"

Ava Wolfe wasn't the type of woman to repeat an opportunity like this again. She would go to the next applicant, repeat the same pitch, and keep going until she found someone willing to give up their life for the job. Elias was twenty-seven years old, uncorrupted, committed, and ready for a challenge. He was so used to cleaning up other people's messes that damage control was part of his routine.

He drew a sharp breath through his nose and shut his portfolio. If he had to give up his life, he wanted to know if it was worth it. "May I ask the remuneration?"

"Of course." She plucked a sheet of paper from her notepad and slid it across the desk toward him. "I hope this figure will sway your decision."

The salary was double what he was getting paid now. "Are you interviewing other candidates?"

Ava smirked. "Is that your subtle way of asking to go forward?"

"Yes, ma'am."

Ava leaned over the table, giving Elias an ample view of the black space between her breasts. "Congratulations, Elias. You're hired," she said as they shook hands. "I assume you'll have to give your employer eight weeks' notice. But we're dealing with a time-sensitive issue here so I need you as soon as possible. Please speak with your employer. Human Resources will be in contact with you again regarding your contract." Ava stood and smoothed her dress down with one hand. "Welcome to Blue Tail Media."

Chapter 3

"Elias, are you there? I'm coming in!" Daisy breezed into Elias's unit early the next morning, jerking him from a deep sleep. He opened one eye, making out the shadowy lines of his bedroom. The blinds were still drawn, casting shadows across the dresser and the pile of clothes strewn helter-skelter around the room.. He ran a hand over his face and sat up in bed, taking in his dishevelled form. He must've had a restless night because his blanket had been pushed to the end of the mattress.

He picked up a shirt from the floor and climbed out of bed. "You can come in, Daisy."

The door exploded inwards as Daisy entered the room, carrying a tray of coffee and a paper bag. She set breakfast down on the dresser and pulled the curtains open, blinding Elias with a beam of bright light. He wandered into the bathroom, keeping the door ajar so he could talk to her.

"So, tell me," she pleaded. "How did the interview go? Did you get the job?"

Elias flushed the toilet and re-emerged in the bedroom, eager to feed his grumbling stomach. Using his forearm, he brushed aside cologne bottles and other knickknacks so they had a makeshift dining table.

Taking a sip of coffee, Elias studied Daisy's excited face. "Didn't I tell you I'd regret giving you a key to my apartment? No one should be this boisterous on a Saturday morning."

She flitted her hand in the air, dismissing his comment.

"You can change the locks another day. Tell me what Ava was like."

Elias thought back to the man-eater in the blue dress, her formidable and predatory personality biting into his resolve. All he could think about were the rumours. When they left the boardroom after the interview, Ava's touch lingered as they shook hands, her body as close to his as it could be, the scent of her perfume wafting in the air. Elias chose not to focus on the glint in her eye, or the way she dragged her tongue across her lips. He just wanted to find another job.

"She was a nice person."

"And?"

He reached for a croissant and took a bite, delaying his answer. "I start as soon as I give notice."

"That's awesome!" Daisy gave him a hug. "I'm so proud of you." She broke the embrace, but remained close, grabbing hold of his wrists. "Do you think you can resist her charm?" A gleam of mischief shone in her eyes.

"Getting this job has nothing to do with Ava or her rumoured reputation. I accepted the job for *me*. No one else. To be honest, I think Ava playing the seductress is just a front. She's lonely and I won't become another one of her conquests." He tossed the croissant onto the dresser and cocked his head to the side, his gaze blazing into Daisy. "Speaking of romance, what's going on with us?" He motioned between them. "My parents eagerly await an engagement announcement that may or may not come. Are we an item or not?"

The colour drained from Daisy's face, replaced with a sombre expression. "Do you think I like throwing subtle hints all the time?" she said, perching on the edge of the bed. "We were together once before. Why can't we try again? I've tried to be civil as your friend, but I want more."

"More what? Romance? We tried that. I broke up with you because it wasn't working out. I decided that remaining friends was the best thing for us. Looks at us. Our relationship is stronger now than when we were together. Why change that?"

She folded her arms across her chest and dipped her chin, a stray lock of blonde hair falling between her eyes. "Elias, how do you feel about me?"

He thrust his hands into his pockets. "I care deeply for you, Daisy. Always have. That will never change."

"In other words, you don't love me."

"I never said that," he said, reaching over to tuck the stray hair behind her ear. "I've been trying to make sense of it for years. You and I are not like normal friends. We're constantly fighting the pull back to each other. I don't know what I want."

"Elias, I cannot wait for you forever. Make a decision before I'm gone for good. You or us." She paused. "To be honest, you accepting this job at Blue Tail makes me nervous." She sucked in a breath and headed for the bedroom door, wrapping her fingers around the knob. "I'm nervous about what kind of person Ava will turn you into. She's a succubus."

"Daisy." Elias voice held an authoritative tone. "That's my new boss you're talking about."

"I'm serious. I'm nervous about losing my best friend." She shot him a pitiful glance before closing the door behind her, leaving Elias bewildered in her wake.

~ ~ ~

Butterflies mixed with coffee cravings as Elias stood in line waiting for his morning cappuccino. The café was buzzing with city workers, chattering loudly, adding more nerves to his tumbling gut. He could see Blue Tail Media's building glistening between the skyscrapers and lost the need for a coffee hit. It was his first day as Ava Wolfe's Director of Communications and he hadn't slept a wink.

His last conversation with Daisy circled in his mind, and he wondered, during his darkest moments of doubt, if she was right—if working with Ms. Wolfe would change him.

"How can I help you?" The barista Gus smiled warmly at him and reached for a takeaway cup stacked up behind him. "Mornin' Elias, the usual today?"

"Yeah, a large cappuccino."

"I haven't seen you around lately," Gus said as he began the ritual of filling the handle with ground coffee beans. "Still with the studio?" His voice was almost drowned out by the noise of the grinder.

"No, I left four weeks ago. I start my new job today."

"Cool, mate. Where at?"

"Blue Tail Media."

The barista filled the takeaway cup with piping hot coffee, the aroma appeasing Elias's anxiety. "Isn't that owned by Ava Wolfe? I heard she bought the company after the baby scandal."

"The very one." Elias paid for his coffee. "Actually, can you tell me if anyone from the company gets their coffee here? It'll be nice to have a point of reference."

Gus's gaze flicked upwards as he tossed the coins into the register. "Yeah, I know a few familiar faces from Blue Tail. I've seen more of a redheaded woman lately."

"Ava Wolfe?"

Gus shrugged. "Could be. There was another girl who came in and mentioned Ava a few times. I haven't seen her in ages though. Did she fire the last girl who got her coffee?"

Elias pressed his lips into a thin line. "Guess so I'm her new Director of Communications."

Gus's eyebrows disappeared into the shaggy hair falling over his forehead. "Seriously? There must be revolving door in there." He smirked at him. "I guess I'll be seeing more of you instead. Good luck today, mate."

"I'll need it." Elias left the café, sipping his coffee, and wandered towards Blue Tail's building. His pace slowed as he neared the office, anxiety getting the best of him. What was he getting himself into? This role could be a career booster or career ender. The question continued to nag him as he stepped into the elevator. He stared at his reflection in the mirror, lips soured, questioning why he wore the red tie with his green suit. His ink-black locks refused to comply, a wave of hair standing up despite the tub of product in it. A detectable five o'clock shadow dusted his strong jawline. He looked half decent, but could've done better. He had looked like a movie star on his first day at Manny Magpie. Was he subconsciously looking bad so Ava wouldn't find him attractive?

The elevator doors opened, and he made direct eye contact with the receptionist. He approached her with a confident smile. "Hello, I'm Elias Dorne. It's my first day."

"Of course. Ava told me you would be starting." She pointed to some chairs lined up against the wall. "Please take a seat. Ava won't be long."

Elias placed his briefcase on the coffee table and sat down, using the time to evaluate his new environment. The office carried an air of positivity and enthusiasm, with music spewing from a radio and staff sharing stories of their weekends. It was nice to know people were friendly around here.

Pretty girls dressed in corporate skirts and blazers, tossed Elias inquisitive stares under long lashes. How many men had sat where he did, wanting a job with the notorious Ava Wolfe?

"Elias, it's nice to finally meet you." A young, dark-haired man appeared from a nearby office, and offered his hand to Elias. "I'm Blake Parker, we spoke on the phone. I'll be showing you around this morning."

Elias gathered his belongings. "I appreciate the opportunity. I look forward to working here."

"You can thank Daisy for the recommendation. She had nothing but positive things to say about you."

As Elias followed Blake through the office, he had one thing on his mind. "Will I be meeting with Ms. Wolfe today?"

"Ava got called out for an urgent meeting this morning, but your area's been set up." He led him through the network of desks and stopped outside a timber door with Ava's name inscribed on a gold plate. "Welcome to your new office."

He opened the door to reveal a clean, crisp room with spectacular views of the Harbour Bridge. Ava's office was professional and white with subtle hints of femininity. A vase of candy-floss pink peonies added some colour to the room. A perfume bottle teetered on the edge of the desk which was positioned by window, giving Ava an awe-inspiring backdrop.

Blake entered the room and pointed to a smaller desk in the corner, adorned with a computer, empty document trays and a cup full of pens and pencils.

"This is your desk. I've left a handful of copy briefs, adverts to approve, and articles to proof read until Ava gets back. She'll go through your job description in more detail. Please take a seat."

Elias wandered to the desk and placed his briefcase on the floor. He sat down and flicked through the paperwork, familiarising himself with the copy and adverts.

"The communal kitchen is down the hall, fully stocked with water and fruit." Blake continued, "I'm two doors down so give me a holler if you need any help with the briefs." He paused when Elias didn't respond, nose deep in his paperwork. "I'll leave you to it. You seem to know what you're doing. The IT department should've left your email and computer password on a sticky note for you."

Elias scanned his desk and found a square piece of paper nudged underneath the keyboard. "Here it is. Thank you, Blake. I'll buzz you if I have any questions."

Elias worked uninterrupted for two hours, listening to the acoustics of the office outside, people talking, music playing. He felt disconnected from his new colleagues already, unable to see them through the frosted glass walls. Blake didn't even introduce him to anyone. First impressions meant more to him than damn advertorials and he would've preferred spending time getting to know everyone. Especially Ava. Was she going to be out of the office all the time? How dependent was she going to be on him?

The office door opened, and Ava entered the room in a flurry of red and green, her mobile phone attached to her ear. She carried a heap of magazines which she dumped on Elias's desk without even looking at him. She wore a tight, green dress, accentuating the copper highlights of her hair.

"I told him the advertisement was running in the December issue," Ava said into the phone. "I have it on email if he's doubting our agreement." She tossed her handbag onto her desk in frustration, her back to Elias as she gazed out the window. "He questions his ad placement every month." She turned around, spotted Elias sitting in his seat and froze. "Frank, I gotta go."

Ava finished the call and lowered her mobile to the desk. "Good morning, Elias." She reached over and shook his hand. "I'm sorry I wasn't here to greet you this morning. I had something urgent to attend to."

He smiled and motioned to the paperwork in front of him. "It's okay, I was covered. Blake gave me some advertorials to write for *Skin Touch Beauty*. I've been working on them this morning."

"Excellent." Ava sat down behind her desk and switched on her computer. "I'll take a look at them later. Did Blake show you around the office and introduce you to everyone?"

"Not yet."

A small smile hooked at her painted lips. "I'll bring you around to the different departments after lunch. I'm sure everyone is keen to meet you." Her grin got wider. "We're a close group here, Elias. I'm hoping you'll fit into our little family."

"I'm a pretty relatable guy, so I hope so too."

Ava flipped open a folder on her desk and sorted through the paperwork. "I'm not sure if you researched the company before your interview and if you did, you would've seen some interesting—and somewhat defamatory—information on Blue Tail. You'll hear certain things about the previous owner and it's important to keep your discretion—if you want to keep your job. Now that you're working under me, you'll attract more interest from my competitors and journalists." She leaned over, her emerald gaze boring into him. "People will confront you. People will judge you. I am confident you can handle it because you're good at your job."

Elias ignored the stab of doubt in his gut. Did he make the right decision accepting this job? He wanted to start over and rebuild a proper career, but how much damage would be done by working with Ava?

"I'm well aware of the risks."

She stood up and wandered to the door. "Why don't I show you around the office now? I would like to take you out to lunch afterwards."

As Ava escorted him through the numerous departments, Elias observed the other staff eying him with a mixture of curiosity and intrigue. He noticed there were more women sitting behind desks than men, so it wasn't surprising he was a figure of interest.

A thought sparked in a deep, roguish part of his brain when he and Ava passed a large mirror leading down the hall. They looked good together, walking side by side, almost hip to hip. With Ava wearing her fancy designer shoes, they were the same height, which he loved in a woman.

"I have multiple titles under the Blue Tail Media umbrella," Ava explained, circumnavigating the Accounts department, shooting quick introductions to the team. "We cater mostly to women's interest but I publish six other titles, including men and lifestyle. I prefer an open window to appeal to every reader in the market."

Elias followed her around, meeting editors, writers, sales, and reception, until they returned to her office where she grabbed her handbag. As they walked outside into the crisp breeze, he looked forward to sharing time with her, one on one. He was keen to unearth this mysterious creature, the woman nicknamed the "man-eater."

Chapter 4

The following three weeks passed by in a blur. Elias spent most of his ten-hour days locked away in Ava's office, working on press releases or attending meetings with the public relations team, discussing ways to tackle the company's poor public image. The scandal was still gathering interest in the media, damaging magazine sales and social media perception.

In the fragile situation Blue Tail Media was in, Elias knew that pumping out repetitive press releases and articles would only have a negative effect in the market. The company's reputation—and his new job—was at stake.

He spent a week of coffee-fuelled nights and hours on the phone booking Ava's appearance on *Day Break*, a popular morning talk show. Interviewing the new CEO of a tainted women's interest media company would not only appeal to the stay-at-home mothers—half of Blue Tail's readership—but would add a feminine touch to a male-dominated industry. Ava was attractive, professional, reserved, and relatable—the perfect antidote to break a viewer's perception. But it would take time and the only thing Elias could do was work as hard as he could to get Ava's face across all Australian television.

He stood in the shadows of the studio lights, watching Ava being interviewed by the host. She looked radiant in her tight-fitting black dress and rosy lips, her shoulder-length hair falling like copper ribbons around her face. She sat on the couch with her long legs curled in front of her, her posture unwavering. If looks had the power to manipulate the public, Blue Tail's magazine sales would soar. Ava's gaze flicked towards him and a barely detectable smile pulled at her lips.

"Your publishing juggernaut Blue Tail Media has a low consumer rating due to the scandal," the host Joel Summers asked, leaning towards Ava with interest. "Everyone wants to know how will you regain buyer trust?"

"Our readership is very important to us," Ava replied. "They are our life blood. Blue Tail Media is a reputable business, topping the ASX list for best Australian company in 2015. I don't want to let our readers down by producing low-quality publications. We have a strong team working behind the scenes listening to customer feedback. In this current age, we are working on shifting our business to meet all digital needs and most importantly, distancing ourselves from the scandal."

"Former employee Lily Harolds filed a class action lawsuit against the company, creating one of the largest scandals Australia has ever seen. You've remained quiet in the press about it. Has there been any developments?"

For a brief moment, Elias saw fear flicker in Ava's eyes. It was the first time he'd seen her show weakness. There was a lot about the scandal that hadn't been released to the media. This was the first time he'd heard about the lawsuit and he wondered how much information Ava had kept from him.

Ava brushed her tongue along her teeth before answering Joel. "I have a reliable and professional legal team who's currently in negotiations with Ms. Harolds regarding her lawsuit. I trust it will be settled outside of court."

"Is it true the board knew of Ms. Harolds before she made the accusations?"

Despite the host's obvious attempt to weaken Ava's resolve, she kept her remarkably unshakable poker face.

"Ms. Harolds was known to the board purely as an employee. I cannot comment for the individuals' personal knowledge of Ms. Harolds."

A subtle look of relief crossed Ava's face when a producer called for an ad break. A makeup artist came on set to touch up her makeup, hovering for a moment to have a quick chat. Elias supposed it was to soften her nerve. The interview wasn't what he expected at all, feeling like it was an attack on Ava personally.

"Are you Ms. Wolfe's new assistant?" A man approached Elias, dressed in a casual T-shirt and jeans, a portable walkie-talkie attached to his hip. His name badge on his lapel read Brent Paterson. "I believe we spoke on the phone."

"No, I'm the new Director of Communications. How many assistants have there been?" Elias joked.

"Too many to count."

Ignoring Brent's dry remark, Elias fished his mobile from his pocket and scrolled through his emails. "Listen, I want to talk to you. The questions your team sent over to me on Monday weren't the ones I had approved. It kinda feels like Joel wants Ava to fail on national television. What the hell is his problem?"

"I'm sorry about that," Brent said. "Trust me, the other producers and I weren't aware he would ask these questions either."

"Why aren't you doing anything about it?"

The man lifted a shoulder. "It makes for great TV."

"Elias!"

He turned when Ava called out his name from her spot on the couch. As he neared, a flicker of concern flashed in her eyes. She wrapped her fingers around his arm, not tightly, however strong enough so he couldn't move.

"Get me out of here," she hissed.

"I don't think you can simply walk out," Elias advised.

"Your interview was booked from ten to ten-thirty." He checked his watch. "It's only ten-fifteen now."

"I don't care. Find an excuse. Tell a producer something came up."

Elias pushed out a breath of air and noticed Joel walking back towards the couch. Live television was unpredictable. Things went wrong all the time. However, how could he justify severing Ava's interview without leaving a shadow on her reputation? Her name alone was associated to the scandal and she wasn't even involved firsthand.

Elias bent down and brushed his lips against her ear. "You need to rebuild the public's trust," he whispered. "I know today hasn't gone to plan, and trust me, I'll be making some waves of my own. But it's important to keep going. It shows the viewers you're able to withstand the tough questions." He paused for a beat. "What I learned from my last job is to feed the public what they want. Give them what they want to hear and it will be over before you know it. Trust me."

She gazed at him doubtfully. "I hired you to help me with public relations. Don't let me down."

"I'm on your side, Ava. I'll always do what's best for you and for the company."

She shot him one of her sly smiles. "If you're right and I make it out of here with my reputation intact, I'm giving you a raise."

An hour later, Elias walked out of the studio able to breathe again. Ava surprised him with her tenacity and grace under pressure, killing the rest of the interview. She exited the set with a renewed bounce in her step like she held the world in the palm of her hand.

He waited for her outside the television studio, holding open the door to her taxi. She came out of the building with her head down, phone plastered to her ear, ignorant to the friendly smile Elias shot her before she slipped into the seats.

He sat beside her, listening to her conversation with one of the editors. Ava had relied on Elias's ingenuity to win back viewers' trust during the interview. Now, she acted like he didn't exist at all, turning away from him in the backseat, knees drawn to the door, her head facing the street. Elias had learned to shake the feeling of neglect. She was his boss. Nothing more.

Besides, he looked forward to having dinner with Daisy tonight. He needed something, someone stable and familiar in his life.

He dug out his tablet from his briefcase and viewed his calendar. Ava finished her phone call and leaned across the seat. "What do I have on this afternoon?"

"You have a meeting at four with an advertising executive from Chanel and a phone conference at six with your accountant."

"Cancel them."

"Excuse me?"

"Cancel them," she echoed, lowering a hand onto his knee, squeezing it. "We've both had a stressful day and I know a great bar down the road. I'm in need of a stiff drink after that ruthless interview." She lifted her hand when his shoulders stiffened. "Do you have plans tonight?"

Elias chewed at his bottom lip, thinking how hard it was to obtain a table at the popular Italian restaurant where he planned to go. "I have dinner reservations at six thirty."

A strange look he couldn't identify crossed Ava's face. "Oh, with your girlfriend?"

"Just a friend."

"Where are you going?"

"Juliana on George Street."

"You'll love it there," Ava gushed. "I know the owners personally and if I'd known you wanted to go, I would've gotten you the best table. But I'm sure it won't matter, anyway.

It's the company that's important, right?" Ava tapped the glass separating them from the driver and relayed directions to the bar. "I won't keep you out for long, I promise."

~ ~ ~

Elias bolted into his apartment at six-fifteen and shed his clothes on the way to the shower. He was running incredibly late. The friendly drink at the bar drew longer than he anticipated, with Ava buying him shots of vodka for two hours. Not wanting to be rude, he accepted each one, feeling the haze of insobriety clouding his brain as he showered. As he pulled on a fresh dress shirt and pants, he sent Daisy a text:

Elias: Running late. Got caught up at work. Be there soon.

He grabbed his wallet and keys off the dresser and dashed for the train. Twenty minutes later, he stumbled into the restaurant out of breath. He spotted Daisy across the room, sitting underneath a dome of lamplight. He could tell by the tautness of her pink lips that she was angry at him.

"I'm sorry I'm late," Elias said as he reached the table, bending down to kiss her cheek. "I had to help an editor put a magazine to print."

"It doesn't matter anymore. Anyway, I took the liberty of ordering entrees," Daisy said at last, reaching for her almost emptied wineglass. "I hope antipasto and bruschetta is okay with you."

"It's fine."

They sat in silence for a few minutes, listening to the soft ambience of the buzzing Italian restaurant. Waiters dressed in black and white uniforms weaved between the tables, holding trays of food and bottles of wine above their heads. An orchestra played the classics from speakers in the corners of the ceiling.

"I saw your boss on *Day Break* today," Daisy said. "She is very beautiful."

"What did you think of the interview?"

"I think the host asked all the right hard-hitting questions. Blue Tail Media has a lot to answer for."

"As a matter of fact, Ava was thrown underneath the bus," Elias argued. "The interview was an attack on her. They didn't ask any of the questions I had approved and—"

"Were you really expecting Ava to appear as the innocent party?" Daisy interjected. "She bought a company fresh from a national scandal. She had to anticipate some curiosity from the media. They're only doing their jobs. I would want to know why a businesswoman purchased a publishing company from a man who allegedly impregnated his young secretary. Did she ever tell you why she bought it?"

"No, it's never come up." He picked up his wine and drained the glass. He didn't want to fight with Daisy. He wanted to talk about their future. When their entrees arrived, he ordered another bottle of red wine and reached for Daisy's hands across the table. "No more talk about work. I want to talk about us."

Her navy eyes softened. "I was surprised you wanted to have dinner on a work night. What's the occasion?"

"There's no occasion. I thought a night out with you was long overdue. We don't hang out as often we used to."

"My life is busy, Elias," Daisy said matter-of-factly. "My job takes up a lot of my time, you know that." She lowered her gaze to the table. "A friendship works both ways, Elias. You can't expect me to organise every coffee date."

"I booked the table, didn't I?" he said with a smile.

"I guess so."

"In fact, I haven't been completely honest with you."

Her eyebrow hooked. "What are you talking about?"

"I asked you out to dinner because I wanted to ask you something."

"Like what?"

He stroked the top of her hand with his thumb. "I don't need any more time to figure us out. I've decided what I want. You, Daisy. You've been the one constant in my life. The one person I can trust. What do you say we give this another try?"

"Oh." Two spots of colour warmed Daisy's cheeks and she slipped her hand out from underneath his. "Where did this come from, Elias? The last time we spoke about our future, you steered the conversation to something else."

"My life is progressing faster than I ever anticipated and I don't want to leave you behind. What do you think?"

Daisy opened her mouth to reply when Elias's mobile phone buzzed in his pocket. Cursing under his breath, he checked the caller ID. It was Ava. He flashed Daisy an apologetic smile. "I have to take this. I won't be long." He dashed outside to answer the call. "Hello, Ava."

"How's your meal?" The soft purr of her voice resonated in his ears.

"Haven't eaten yet. How can I help you?"

"I need you to do a favour for me. I received a call from Otto Shop and they have our cheque ready. Tony's keeping the shop open until seven-thirty. Do you think you can swing by and pick it up? It's not far from Juliana."

Elias checked his watch. It was seven o'clock already. He glanced back into the restaurant and saw Daisy sitting in her chair, twirling a lock of hair around her finger. By accepting Ava's offer, he knew that he would have to be available outside of work hours too, but tonight was meant to be a fresh start with Daisy. In retrospect, he should've turned his phone off.

"Our mains haven't arrived yet, Ava," Elias replied carefully. "Is it possible for Otto Shop to remain open until eight? I can't just leave my date."

She sighed into the phone. "Elias, it would make my life easier if you could go over tonight. Account's been chasing them for payment for months. Can you do it for me?" She paused and then added under her breath, "I know it's a lot to ask."

Elias pinched the bridge of his nose. The clothing store was three blocks away. He could walk there and make it back to Daisy in under twenty minutes. "All right. I'll go."

"Thank you, Elias," Ava said before she hung up.

When Elias returned to his table, a steaming plate of lamb shanks and vegetables was waiting for him. He pulled out his seat but didn't sit down. "I have to go," he announced, grabbing his jacket off the back of the chair.

"What do you mean?"

"Ava's asked me to run an errand."

"Now? You're off duty."

"I know, and unfortunately I'm on a time frame." His stomach grumbled at the rustic aroma of his meal and he regretted saying yes to Ava. "I'll be back soon."

Daisy sat back in her chair and pushed her plate aside, her jaw squared with disappointment. "Your meal will be cold when you get back. Where exactly are you going?"

"I have to pick up a cheque from a client."

Daisy's eyebrows snapped together. "How did Ava know you were in the city? Did you tell her where we were having dinner tonight?"

"It was bought up in friendly conversation, Daisy. She *is* my boss. Look, I don't want to argue. I'll be back soon." As soon as Elias departed the restaurant into the crisp night, he was certain that Ava would be the woman who would come between them.

Chapter 5

Ava drew a calming breath and wished the jug of ice water in front of her was filled with merlot. Her resentment for early-morning meetings was deep rooted from years of working with the same misogynists on the board. She was the only woman at the table, making it hard for her voice to be heard over the testosterone.

She crossed her legs and waited for the chatter to die down. Sitting at the head of the table, she had the perfect view of everyone in the room. Lined on either side of her were pompous, overweight, and overpaid executives of the Blue Tail Media company. The board meeting was called to discuss the *Day Break* interview which had become viral on social media. The air buzzed with a coupling of excitement and concern.

Ava picked up her empty water glass, striking the bottom against the table like a gavel. The entire room stilled. "Gentlemen, can we please get back to the matter at hand?" she said calmly. Once the grumbling had settled down, she continued. "I learned today that I've gained notoriety on Facebook after my interview on *Day Break*. As I don't follow social media trends, can anyone tell me why my face is all over the Internet?"

"You're trending," Gary Trope interjected, an executive who sat on her left. "The interview was a success. As they say, any publicity is good publicity. The aftermath of the scandal left a dark cloud over the company and no matter what we tried—advertisements, billboards, or radio ads— nothing seemed to remove the stink. But your appearance on

Day Break worked." He flipped open a folder in front of him. "Our stocks have gone up, magazine sales have increased by ten percent, and followers on all of our social media platforms have doubled."

"I was ridiculed and humiliated," Ava pointed out. "If I had known they were going to attack me on live television, I would've told the producers to go screw themselves."

"The Australian people love the underdog," Gary said. "I'll admit the interview's direction was unexpected but the viewers responded well to your appearance. You have humility and poise under pressure."

"I own two Fortune 500 companies, including this one," Ava replied forcefully. "All the media wants to hear about is the scandal. Blue Tail has been brandished with a legacy of ill repute, deceit, and a CEO who couldn't keep it in his pants. I don't know about you, but Bobbie Hayes has a lot to answer for."

Gary glanced at the others around him. "We don't regret appointing you CEO, Ava. You've achieved more for this company than Hayes ever did. As a women's interest magazine, we had a certain reputation to uphold. We were compelled to offer Hayes a clean resignation before shit hit the fan. I don't regret doing it."

"But shit *did* hit the fan," Ava said. "Aren't you forgetting Lily Harold's lawsuit? Can you update me on the progress with that? I promised the public on live television that we are in negotiations."

Gary cleared his throat. "Our legal team has it under control."

"So what's the result?" Ava persisted. "Am I going to be out of pocket hundreds of thousands of dollars to keep our name out of the mud again?"

"Ms. Harolds insists on going to court to pursue her class action." Gary put his hands up defensively when Ava's shoulders stiffened. "But our lawyers are working on a deal to clear the waters."

"Look, I understand where she's coming from," Ava said. "She's hurting and angry. She trusted her employer, who in turn, violated her body, ending in pregnancy. I would be after blood too if I was in her position." Ava flicked a stray lock of copper hair from her face. "What about the other girls?"

"Excuse me?"

"Do you think I'm a stupid woman, Gary? I know about Hayes's other victims. How much did you pay them to keep them quiet?"

"There was only one: Lily Harolds."

Ava blew out a breath of hot air and picked up a remote, activating the projector screen behind her head. As she spoke, she flicked through photographs of young women in the park, sitting at bus stops, at the store, or driving to work. "Bobbie Hayes was a womaniser and preferred pretty and fertile prey. What you see on the screen are the women caught in his web. Six working-class girls, barely out their teens were hired by Hayes to work as his PA. They were desperate for a career and a well-paying job so they were willing to do anything"—she switched off the projector—"anything for a dollar." She poured herself a glass of water, relishing the stillness of the room. She reminded herself to rebuild her board one day with women. "In fact, I'm surprised they haven't come forward. So, please enlighten me on how much money we're paying these women to stay quiet."

A soft murmur rippled down the table and Gary grew incredibly uncomfortable, fidgeting in his seat. "After Lily came forward to the media, we were confronted by a handful of other women in the same situation. Before you were appointed, the company was in limbo. There was too much to lose if we let those girls to come forward."

"So, you concealed the victims from the new CEO?"

"It was for the company's protection, Ava. When you took over Blue Tail Media, we became profitable again for the first time in years. The board decided that we couldn't risk the identities of the women getting out, destroying our reputation." He inhaled a breath. "We settled with each woman outside of court quietly."

"How many children are involved?"

"I believe there are five."

Ava shook her head in disbelief. She understood the gamble when buying a company drowning in scandal and, in hindsight, she probably should've listened to her solicitor. But Blue Tail Media was her responsibility and she wasn't ready for the publishing giant to crumble into dust. Not yet.

"Has anyone been in contact with Lily recently?" she asked. "Surely this girl knows what's involved in pursuing a case like this. All her deep dark secrets would be exposed. She must think of her child."

"What are you proposing?" Gary asked tentatively.

"I say we move forward and keep producing high-quality magazines. That's what we're here for, aren't we? Our readers expect the best and despite the slump in sales, Blue Tail is still number one in the market. I'm relying on you and your legal team to ensure Ms. Harolds's settlement is clean. I'm presuming the settlement will include a clause so she cannot discuss the case outside her legal team?"

Gary nodded. "Ms. Harolds is prohibited from making public statements about the case. If she speaks to anyone in the company, we have the right to sue and force the money to be returned."

Ava gathered her things and slid them into her bag. "I'm happy to hear you have everything under control, Gary." She checked her mobile, flicking her gaze upwards for a fleeting second. "That's why I hired you. Now, I have a company to run."

Fuelled by a surge of confidence, Gary referred to his own notes, stopping Ava from leaving her chair. "If you're so confident with moving on, what can you tell me about Elias Dorne? You're paying him an eye-watering wage. What has he done specifically to boost our brand? As you said, our sales are poor for this time of year and the *Day Break* interview was the only appearance I've seen. The board wants answers. Why are we paying big dollars for someone who hasn't shown his worth?"

"It's what *I'm* paying him," Ava corrected. "Elias came very highly recommended. Do you remember the Manny Magpie scandal a few months back?"

Gary nodded. "The ice addict who went berserk on a kid's show. Yeah, I saw it."

"Do you recall how quickly it got swept underneath the rug? It was page one news for maybe a week or two. The studio was back on the air before anyone noticed it was off." Ava smiled proudly. "That was Elias. It was his job to rebuild Manny Magpie's reputation. You see, Elias is very skilled in dealing with scandals and getting a company back on its feet. I'm confident he will do the same for us." She cocked her head to the side. "Does that answer your question, Gary?"

He looked unsure but conceded, "Yes, Ava."

~ ~ ~

Elias watched the sun gradually sink behind the skyscrapers, bathing the sky in a rich palette of orange and fuchsia pink. He rubbed his eyes with the ball of his palms, hoping when he opened them, the stash of paperwork in front of him would mysteriously disappear.

"I need to approve the updated testimonials from our advertisers." Ava sat opposite him, a glass of sherry at arm's reach, her emerald dress crinkle-free despite the late hour. "Do you have them?"

Elias chewed at his bottom lip, eyeing Ava's tumbler of alcohol greedily, wishing he was on a train heading home to watch the football. "Yes, I do. They were quite forthcoming in giving them to me." He handed her a document buried underneath his empty coffee cup. "I've gathered ten testimonials from our biggest advertisers. With your approval, the IT team will put them on the website tonight."

"I knew I could rely on my loyal advertisers," Ava said, reading the endorsements with a timid smile. "We lost a lot of clients when the Hayes scandal hit the media and the list is slowly rebuilding. When I was appointed, I bought a portfolio of clients over with me from my last company. They're the ones that kept us afloat when the scandal became public." She reached for her drink with cherry-red nails. "Elias, I want you to keep monitoring as much as you can. Search social media, hashtags, YouTube videos, and news outlets for any mention of our name. While customers may accept our apology, negative feedback can still cripple a company. I'm hoping these testimonials you've gathered will be another building block."

While Ava got up to refill her glass at the liquor cabinet built into the bookshelf, Elias stole a glance at his mobile. He had multiple texts from Daisy asking when he was coming home. He'd forgotten she planned a night in with a DVD and Chinese takeaway. His poor attempt of being a good boyfriend was yet another breakable facet in their relationship.

"Am I keeping you from something?" Ava asked, returning to the table.

Elias tucked his phone into his pocket hurriedly. "Just my girlfriend. We had a date tonight."

"You can go if you want to," Ava offered as she checked her slim gold watch. "It's seven-thirty. I never intended to keep you back this long, but I think we made some progress."

Elias nodded in agreement and pushed his chair back. "I think so too. Do you recommend any good florists that are open at this hour? If I'm one more minute late, I'll have to beg for mercy from Daisy."

Interest piqued in Ava's emerald eyes. "How long have you been together?"

"Not long, but Daisy and I have known each other since we were kids. We went to school and university together. It took almost fifteen years for me to realise how I felt about her."

"Trust me, Elias, you will want to get back into her good graces right away. Petals on Margaret is my favourite florist," Ava answered, downing her sherry. "They sell exotic flowers you won't find anywhere else in the city. Call them before you leave so Jodie can stay open for you. I think the receptionist has the business card." She got up from her chair and left the room, leaving the door ajar.

As he watched Ava's silhouette disappear into the dark office, Elias pulled out his phone and shot a quick text to Daisy.

Elias: I'll be home in thirty. I'm sorry.

Not expecting a reply, he pocketed his mobile and waited for Ava to return, anxiously biting at his fingernails. An insistent buzzing sounded from underneath a pile of paperwork, attracting his gaze. Elias pushed everything aside to reveal Ava's ringing mobile. The name *Liam Heathcote* appeared on the screen. Recognising the name as one of the company's top advertisers, Elias wondered if he should answer it. Ava would often push her phone in his direction if she was too busy to take a call.

He leaned over in his chair, unable to see her at reception. "Ava, your phone is ringing."

"Answer it," she called from the front of the office. "I'll be there soon."

Hesitantly, he obeyed, answering the vibrating mobile. "Ava Wolfe's phone."

"I'm after Ava."

"She's unable to take your call right now. Can I take a message?"

"Who's this?" demanded a strong male voice on the other end.

"I'm the Director of Communications," Elias repeated. "Can I take a message?"

"Where is she?"

"Not here." Elias grimaced at his indirect response but he was tired and wasn't in the mood for rude callers. "She's away from her desk at the moment. May I ask who's calling so she can ring you back?"

"I'll phone her later tonight."

Ava entered the room as the man hung up and handed Elias a business card. "I gave the florist a call. Jodie will remain open until eight so you better get going."

"That's very nice of you. I'll head off now." Elias handed Ava her mobile. "A man named Liam Heathcote called. He said he'll ring you back tonight. Is he the same Liam of Heathcote PR?"

Ava blew out a breath and tossed the phone onto the desk "Yes, Liam is also my ex-husband."

Chapter 6

Ava manoeuvred her Mercedes into the driveway and groaned with grievance at the sight of Liam's black Audi parked outside the garage. The chandeliers in the foyer were on, throwing fractured light onto the stone entryway. Disembodied music spewed from the open windows.

Ava bit back a curse as she gathered her things and shut the car door with her hip, regretting the day she gave Liam a spare key. She entered the house and charged for the kitchen where she found him at the stovetop, cooking a meal.

"What are you doing here?" she demanded, throwing her handbag and keys onto the marble bench. "We're not married anymore, remember?"

Tapping the wooden spoon against the pot, Liam turned an eye at her. "Yeah, I remember, but the sex is better now than when we were married."

Ava perched a hand on her hip. "Is that why you're here? Looking for a booty call?"

Liam wandered to the fridge and helped himself to a bottle of wine. "I don't know what I want anymore, Ava." He filled two wineglasses and slid one across the bench towards her. "I wanted to surprise you with a nice home-cooked meal." He jerked his thumb over his shoulder. "I saw the empty takeaway containers in the bin. Don't you shop for real food anymore?"

"I don't have time to cook," Ava replied, tossing back the glass of alcohol. "I work fourteen-hour days. I have companies to run." She sat down on a bar stool and watched him dish out steaming stir fry into bowls. "Why did you call this afternoon? I was busy."

A sneer pulled at Liam's lips. "Funny you should bring that up. Who's the new boy toy answering your phone? I thought you only hired girls."

"I hired girls because you got jealous when I employed males. You thought I was screwing them in my office."

Liam's green eyes narrowed. "You did."

Ava slammed her palm down on the bench. "It was one time, Liam. A tiny indiscretion."

"An indiscretion that ruined our marriage." Liam spooned a forkful of noodles into his mouth. "So what's your new assistant's name?"

"Elias, and he's more than my assistant."

"Is that all you're going to tell me? Am I forbidden to know his background or even his bloody surname?" Liam tossed his fork into the plate, the silver echoing painfully against the crockery. "Are you fucking him?"

"I haven't touched him!" Ava shouted, pushing her chair back. She glared at her ex-husband and welcomed a rush of disgust. "How dare you make assumptions. I'm not that kind of woman anymore." She abandoned her dinner on the bench and stormed up the stairs towards her bedroom.

Liam hastily followed, shouting after her, "Don't you walk away from me, Ava. We haven't finished talking." He confronted her as she headed for the ensuite, grabbing her arm and jerking her body against his. "What's going on with you?"

Ava matched his stare with determined ferocity. "There's nothing going on between my employee and me."

"That's not what I meant," Liam said. "What's going with *you*? You used to like my unannounced visits." He ran his hand through his short-cropped hair. "We used to be so deeply in love."

"Love doesn't exist," she spat, slipping from his grip. "We are divorced, Liam. Our relationship is over. We spend way too much time together for people who're no longer in love."

"We can still be friends, can't we?"

"The friends with benefits clause you rely on so much is over." Ava wandered to the bathroom but didn't go inside, her fingers wrapped around the knob. "Why did you call me today? It couldn't be for ad placement. Your agency is booked up for the rest of the year."

Liam approached her and slipped one arm around Ava's waist. When she didn't object, he moved in closer, chest to chest. "I called your mobile because I wanted to see you outside of the office." He was brave enough to steal a sneaky kiss. "To spend time with you." Ava was motionless when he peeled off her clothes, allowing herself to succumb to her ex-husband's charms. When she stood naked in his arms, feeling exposed and vulnerable, she shut her eyes, hating how lonely she'd become since their divorce. Liam was a warm body, nothing more.

"Are you seeing anyone?" Liam murmured as he feathered kisses along her jawline.

"No. Are you?"

Moaning under his breath, Liam carried her to the bed and climbed on top of her, shredding his shirt and pants in the process. "I'm seeing a twenty-year-old," he said in between kisses. "She works at the account agency in my office building."

Ava inhaled a sharp breath when he entered her body. She fell into rhythm with him, her head lopped to one side, staring at the pile of paperwork on her nightstand, thinking how she was going to finish it if Liam stayed the night. When he climaxed inside her, Ava didn't linger for the post-sex pleasantries. She wandered into the bathroom and shut the door behind her, spending twenty minutes washing Liam's scent off her. When she re-entered the bedroom, she found him asleep on his side of the bed, naked, the sheet covering the curve of his hip. As she studied his strong profile and muscular frame, he reminded her of what their relationship used to be—boring, monotonous, and safe. Ava couldn't deny she had loved Liam wildly, but she craved something more fulfilling—like her career.

Too tired to kick Liam out, Ava dressed into her pajamas and slipped into the silk sheets, hoping she could fall asleep without the normal thoughts of work keeping her awake.

~ ~ ~

Elias wished his co-worker Scott Parish would stop bothering him and get back to work. The young man perched on the edge of Elias's desk, scrolling through photos of his crazy weekend on his phone. His boyish face was alit with glee.

"Oh, you have to see this one, mate," he said, shoving the mobile under his nose. "See that hot chick with her arm around me?"

"Yeah."

"She had the best rack I'd ever seen!" he said unabashedly, his grin getting wider. "I buried my face in it all night." His cheeks then reddened. "In fact, there was another part of her I buried deep into."

Elias blew out a frustrated breath and minimised the document window on his computer screen. "Scott, this is hardly a conversation for the office. Do you have work to do? Because I can gladly give you some. Ava will be returning from her meeting at any moment, so get out of her office."

"It's all work and no play with you, isn't it?" Scott replied glumly, slipping his mobile back into his pocket. "You never come out for drinks with us after work. All you do is sit in this office and type on your laptop until the sun goes down."

"I enjoy working here, Scott, and I would like to keep it that way."

"You've been here for a month, right?"

Elias nodded.

"How's Ava been treating you?" Scott wiggled his fingers at Fiona, a staff writer, as she walked towards the copy machine. "During my first week, I thought having a female boss would mean laid-back Mondays and casual Fridays. But Ava's just as hard-ass and cunning as some of her male counterparts. She needs to have control over *everything*. I thought CEOs sat in their big, airy offices drinking scotch and smoking cigars all day."

"Not Ava. She fought tooth and nail for this company and still does. I understand why she needs oversight," Elias said. "Blue Tail Media is a juggernaut in the industry but we're still brushing the dirt off our shoulders after this scandal. Ava is being careful of every word the company publishes at the moment. Everyone is watching us, scrutinising us. One wrong move and this company—and your job—is gone."

Scott rubbed the back of his neck. "I didn't realise it was that bad. Has she disclosed all of this to you? She's a very private person. I doubt she's told the board half the stuff that goes through her crazy head. Did you know you're the first male assistant she's had in three years?"

"I'm not her assistant. But I've heard the rumours." Elias sat back in his chair, arms crossed over his chest. "Is that why I was getting inquisitive stares on my first day?"

Scott nodded. "Yes, but most of the girls in the office think you're hot."

"I'm already spoken for."

Scott checked his watched and cleared his throat. "Well, I better get back to my desk. I told Angela I was getting a coffee thirty minutes ago." He turned to leave when his cheeky smile returned. "Look, here comes Ms. Wolfe now. You better watch out, Elias. She has *that* look in her eye."

Elias glanced up and saw Ava enter the reception area, her unwavering gaze fixed on him. She wore a crisp white blouse, black pencil skirt, and crimson-red heels that matched the hue of her lips. Her copper curls bounced with every step.

Scott slipped out of her office just as she entered, brushing past his shoulders. "Good afternoon, Scott," she said. "What are you doing in my office? I hope you're not dragging Elias from his work?"

Scott's entire face flushed pink and he shuffled on his feet nervously. "I was just giving him a copy brief for *Storm* magazine. I'm leaving now." He darted out of the room, closing the door behind him.

Ava heaved her handbag and a pile of magazines onto her desk. She sat down with a huff, dragging her hand through her windswept hair. "Sometimes I wonder if I hired the wrong salesman. All Scott seems to do is float around the office looking for accomplices." She reached for the cappuccino placed on her desk before her arrival. "Despite Scott's visit, did you get any work done?"

"Do you want me to leave out Scott's debaucheries?"

A playful sneer pulled at Ava's lips. "Please do."

Elias picked up his notepad and read through his list. "All press releases have been written, edited, and scheduled for release. I've booked journalists from the *Herald*, the *Star* and the *Sydney Sun* to interview you over the next fortnight. I've corresponded with *Bespoke Public Relations* and their media buying team to purchase advertising space in—"

"Stop right there," Ava interjected, putting her hand up. "Cancel all future advertising with *Bespoke* as of today. I haven't been happy with their services for a while. They don't have the skill base to handle our hefty requirements, especially after the scandal. From now on, I want you to work closely with Heathcote PR regarding upcoming advertising and promotion. They are experts in brand awareness and rebuilding public trust."

Elias struggled to keep up with the words pouring from Ava's lips, jotting everything down on a notepad. "I'm aware that Heathcote PR is an advertiser," he said, "but why haven't we used them for public relations before?"

Ava's red lips thinned as she scrolled through her unread emails. "Our business relationship was complicated, but I anticipate solid results with this agency. They're very good at what they do."

All Elias could think of was Ava's ex-husband and the unwelcome jolt of jealousy in his gut. "Do you want me to arrange a meeting with Mr. Heathcote this week?"

Ava spun her wrist around to check her watch. "No, today. I told him you would be at his office at four o'clock. It's three-thirty and the school kids are out. Get your ass on the next train."

Chapter 7

Casually lounging back in his leather chair, Liam Heathcote eyed Elias across the desk with a cool, cat-like nonchalance. Dressed like James Bond and built like an athlete with wide shoulders, long legs, and a strong jawline, Liam fit very nicely into the black and gold décor of his office. Awards and accolades adorned the walls and if Elias angled his head right, he could see an old photo of Liam and Ava's wedding tucked between the dust-coated knickknacks on the book shelf.

"Would you like a drink?" Liam offered, gesturing towards a mini fridge against the wall. "I have beer and vodka."

Elias shook his head politely, wishing he'd bought a scarf to combat the air conditioner stationed above his head. Any sweat patches on his body from the train ride had now dried. "No, thank you. Maybe some other time."

Liam swung one leg over the other and squeezed a stress ball in one hand, his green eyes narrowing slightly. "I can't trust a man who doesn't drink during the day." He threw the ball across the room where it rolled underneath the couch. "Anyway, I want to discuss the work you did for the Manny Magpie scandal. Ava told me how you single-handedly bought the studio back from the brink. She's very impressed."

"What man doesn't like a woman telling him how brilliant he is?" Elias quipped.

Liam tossed his head back and laughed. "Quite true, mate. You would be a great fit for my agency. I need people with sharp wit and instinct. It's a shame Ava snapped you up before I had a chance."

"I don't think Ava would let me go for anyone."

A shadow of jealousy flashed across Liam's face and Elias wondered if he'd struck a nerve. He knew the man was intimidated by him because he was working closely with his ex-wife every day. Elias figured the wedding photo on the shelf was a gesture of false hope to rekindle their relationship.

"Ava's a tough bird," Liam added as he walked over to the bar fridge to extract a bottle of beer. "When Bobbie Hayes was kicked out, General Manager Chris Smith, a Hayes loyalist, resigned the same week, leaving Ava to clean up his mess. She's working two jobs to keep the company afloat. That's why she hired you, Elias." Liam jarred a finger at him. "Her concerns should be about getting Blue Tail Media out of the gossip pages and back into the public's good graces."

"That's why I'm here, isn't it?" Elias asked, thinking he should've opted for a beer after all. "What do you have in mind?"

Liam sat back down, taking a swig. "I'm thinking a good, old-fashioned charity fundraiser could restore the company's image. It worked for Sky Airlines after their disastrous PR fail and boosted Malik Bank's shares when their CEO was caught in a brothel. The business world is rife with scandal. But it's never the end of the world. If a company can survive public backlash, it can survive anything." Liam tapped his fingers on his desk in absent thought. "We can raise money for breast cancer awareness or domestic violence. The public associates Blue Tail with Hayes and we want to erase that stigma. I know a great charity called SHE who helps DV victims get back on their feet."

"What do you want me to do?"

"Ava would want this event to be front-page news. It's our job to make that happen. Since you and I'll be working closely together, we need to think on the same page. No bullshit, no hierarchy," Liam explained. "We can brainstorm later on. For now, get on the phone and contact every high-end hotel in the city. Due to the scandal, it might take some persuading to get interest, but we'll keep going. The Pameer Hotel's Grand Ballroom might be a good place to start. Let's see if they would be willing to accommodate our requests." Liam leaned forward in his chair.

"It's very important we get this right, Elias. The entire company is teetering on the edge and I want to pull it back from the brink. I'm positive this event will be a hit. Most of all, Ava is relying on us to make it work. She's an attractive, high-visibility CEO trying to bring some stability and growth back to Blue Tail Media. As hard and tiresome as the job is, she never gets a break, ever. If she were an unattractive man in a bad suit, she'd be a hero to the public. She's a woman. It makes everything worse, but it's my job to make it better."

"I agree with you, Liam. Blue Tail's still in damage control," Elias said. "If the fundraiser fails, it's not just Ava's head on the chopping block. When should I book a room?"

"The sooner the better. We need to send out invitations as soon as possible. Book something within six weeks. Can you do that? It doesn't give you a lot of time. Most places book out six to twelve months in advance."

Elias was very good at his job. In the past, he had booked conferences, meetings, and concerts with less notice. He could do anything. The competitive side of him wanted to prove to Liam he was a solid adversary. "I'm on it."

Finishing his drink, Liam wandered to the bar fridge again. "Can I interest you in a beer, Elias? You look like a man who could loosen up a bit."

The clock above Liam's head ticked over to six thirty. Elias was eager to get home and showered. A month working at Blue Tail Media had already isolated him from family and friends. Was it really worth it? He pushed his chair back and slipped into his jacket. "Thanks, but no thanks. I have plans tonight. I'll email you a list of hotels tomorrow."

~ ~ ~

"Elias, how are you enjoying your new job?" Donald Henderson asked as he took a swig of his beer. "Daisy told us you're working extra hard these days."

Elias swallowed the chunk of prawn in his mouth and ignored the disapproval dripping from the man's lips. For years, Elias's career had come first, always, instilled in him at an early age by his parents. *Work hard to earn the things you want.* Elias lived by their mantra—owning his first apartment and a brand-new sports car, which he never drove, before he was twenty. When he was younger, success mattered more than love. Past girlfriends had left him out of frustration, angered by his absence in the relationship. It was never intentional—Elias just loved working.

Now, as he sat opposite the astute Mr. Henderson, watching the corner of his lips twitch in distaste, Elias knew the former policeman would be analysing every word he said.

"I'm enjoying my job very much, sir," he replied, swirling his fork around his creamy prawn fettuccine. "It can be demanding at times, but there's more career direction with this employer. At the moment, I'm organising a charity fundraiser. We're hoping it will be the biggest event of the year." In fact, working with Liam, organising the fundraiser meant he saw more sunrises than he saw his girlfriend. He was failing big time as her boyfriend, and unfortunately Daisy knew it too. She sat next to him, rigid as a post, her cherry-red lips pressed into a thin line, burying her fork into her pasta. Whether she was mad at him or at her father's interrogation, Elias was unsure.

Donald cleared his throat and reached for his beer bottle. "I imagine it will be."

"Who will be attending the fundraiser?" interjected Olivia, Daisy's mother, who sat beside her husband. Her eyes were wide with interest, glistening. "Have you invited any movie stars or television celebrities to the fundraiser?"

Another perk of working in the media was the occasional bumping into famous people at events. Elias had met well-known actors, philanthropists, politicians, and musicians over the years. They were just like normal people. He didn't understand society's obsession with celebrity.

"I'm working with a PR company to organize the invite list. We have a few names on there you may recognise." He flashed her a smile, dropping it immediately when he saw a muscle tick in Donald's jaw. He was getting sick of the constant battle to impress Daisy's folks. Unless he put a ring on her finger, he would forever be the pariah. He knew he should've hosted the dinner at home, that way he would be in his own territory, but Daisy insisted the one-hour drive to her parents' was important.

Then, his mobile phone vibrated in his pocket, giving him a brief respite. He took the opportunity to grab the empty crystal jug on the table. "I'll fill this up," he announced, crossing the room to the kitchen. As he turned on the cold water, he checked the text message. It was from Ava:

Guess who's coming to the fundraiser? Teddy Rollins!

There was Olivia's movie star. The Sydney-born Hollywood actor was the famous face Elias needed to bring the cameras and paparazzi to the event. Teddy was still riding the wave of success after winning his first Academy Award this year. The press followed him everywhere.

Elias texted back:

How did you do to persuade him to come?

Ava replied immediately:

We dated in high school. He owed me one after I got his first audition in Hollywood. Teddy is a good friend and he'll accept any publicity right now. Having a recent Oscar winner attending the event means we can charge more for the raffle tickets.

Elias heard a chair scrape across the floor in the dining room and he quickly pocketed his phone. Daisy entered the kitchen with a stack of plates in her hands.

"Are you coming back to the table or are you going to stay here and text your boss all night?" she asked, slotting the plates into the dishwasher.

"How did you know it was Ava?" he asked, resting a hip against the counter, arms crossed over his chest.

"You practically left a smokey outline of your body when you ran from the table. I don't know anyone else who gets the same reaction from you. What did she want?"

"She texted to say she booked the fundraiser's guest of honour. That was all."

Fuelled by the five glasses of wine in her belly, Daisy went on a tirade, her pale eyes turning a shade of black. "You can't take one night off, can you? We came here to see my parents and have family time, but you still brought your work phone. You drop everything for Ava Wolfe."

"I'm the Director of Communications," Elias interjected. "I'm on call twenty-four/seven. You knew of this when I signed the dotted line."

Daisy paced the kitchen back and forth, growing more agitated with each step. "I've tried to be lenient and accepting of your late nights and *work* dinners. There are two people in this relationship, Elias, not three." She stopped and spun around, shoving a finger in his face. "Are you sleeping with her?"

In his peripheral vision, Elias made out the profile of Daisy's parents sitting at the table, their heads angled a certain way to eavesdrop on their conversation. He clasped Daisy's elbow and pulled her out of sight.

"I'm not sleeping with Ava nor will I ever," he rasped. "She's my boss. I'm getting paid the big bucks to be at her beck and call whenever she needs me, including the nights we have dinner at your parents. Okay? I've worked too hard to leave this job because my girlfriend is jealous."

Daisy's eyebrows snapped together. "I never said I was."

"It's clear you are. Why are you so intimidated by her?"

Her shoulders sagged. "I don't know if I can trust her around you. She's a man-eater, Elias. I've read the articles about her conquests in trash magazines."

"That's what they are. TRASH!" Elias hardly recognised the explosive voice that spewed from his lips. He wished he never said anything at all, especially when Daisy cowered in surprise.

Donald barged into the kitchen, armed with a ferocious expression. "What's going on in here?" His eyes lowered to Elias's fingers wrapped around Daisy's wrist. "Are you all right, Daisy?"

Elias didn't wait for her to answer. He stormed out of the kitchen and headed for the front door. He pried it opened and wandered the streets, burning footprints into the pavement. He was trembling with rage. Daisy could drive home without him. At this moment, fuelled by a cocktail of embarrassment, anger, and regret, Elias refused to be with her. Jealousy was an ugly beast that tore apart relationships. Ava meant nothing to him. Right?

As if on cue, his mobile phone rang in his pocket. It was Ava. When he answered, he buried his emotions deep. He vented his frustration by kicking at the grass lining the footpath. "Evening, Ava."

"Elias, have I caught you at a bad time?"

"No," he replied bluntly.

"Oh, good." She paused. "Have you arranged the entertainment for the fundraiser yet?"

"No."

"I have an idea. Teddy Rollins is on board so we need the get talent to match. The event needs live music, not the crap they play at the mall. Get in contact with record companies around Sydney and start booking their clients. Live music creates a comfortable environment and encourages people to spend more. Don't forget to include Liam as he has—" A truck flew passed, swallowing up her last words. "Where are you?"

"On the side of the road."

"Why? I thought you were going up the coast to see Daisy's folks."

"We have. I'm walking to the bus stop right now because she and I had a fight."

"Elias, that's a little foolish, don't you think? Give her a call to apologise."

"Why? I did nothing wrong. Plus, I think her father would kill me. I shouted at his daughter."

Ava's low, hearty laugh sent a bittersweet warmth throughout Elias's body. "You are so stubborn," she said. "Do you want me to pick you up?"

"I'm an hour outside of Sydney. Besides, if I turn around now, I'll be back at Daisy's in fifteen minutes."

"Elias, I can't tell you how many times I've been in your position. When I was married to Liam, we fought like cats and dogs. One of us would usually storm out and spend a night at a hotel. Giving yourself time to cool off will clear your mind and conscience. I can pick you up."

"Aren't you in the city?"

"No, I drove up the coast Saturday morning for a meeting and I'm heading back now. I'm only thirty minutes away. My offer still stands."

Elias stopped in his tracks, staring into the enveloping darkness surrounding him. Golden headlights fleeted by, throwing beams of light onto the pavement. He could turn around and face the music—and Donald—at Daisy's house or he could accept Ava's lift and sleep in his own bed tonight. There was no point dwelling on his actions, as long as his ride home with Ava was kept secret.

"Okay," he said at last. "Where should I meet you?"

"There's a petrol station on Faulkner Street. Do you think you can meet me there?"

"Sure. And thanks."

When Ava hung up, Elias sent a quick text to Daisy:

Elias: Catching a train home. I need time to cool off. Don't worry. I'll talk to you tomorrow.

Chapter 8

"Do you need me to pick you up afterwards?" Daisy asked as she drove through the late evening traffic towards the charity fundraiser. "I don't mind waiting in the car."

Elias smoothed out a wrinkle in his three-hundred-dollar suit and tossed her a sideways smile. "No, you don't need too. The company has arranged a hotel room for the night. It will be a late one. The last band doesn't perform until eleven." He patted her knee. "Go out to dinner with your friends or crash at my place. I'll see you in the morning."

Elias had returned home Sunday night to his favourite six-pack of beer cooling in the fridge and a naughty DVD on top of his player in the bedroom. Whenever they fought, Daisy was always diplomatic, practically on her knees begging for forgiveness. She was terribly predictable that way, so Elias took pleasure knowing she would do anything to get him back.

"I expect you to send a million selfies with Teddy Rollins tonight," Daisy said, glancing at herself in the rearview mirror. "I'm devastated I won't be able to meet him." She inspected her makeup-free face with an evident look of self-loathing. She dropped her hand from her cheeks and turned to him. "Will Ms. Wolfe be attending tonight?"

"Of course she will be," Elias said. "She organised the event."

Daisy dragged her bottom lip through her teeth. "Elias, please . . ." She stopped herself before saying the words he knew she was thinking. *Please behave. Please don't drink too much. Please don't cheat on me.*

"I'll call you when I'm in my hotel room," he promised, leaning forward to press a soft kiss on her mouth. "I'll text you if it's not too late, okay?" He could feel the self-doubt rolling off Daisy in waves as he opened the car door and exited into the crisp night. He leaned into the open window. "I'll see you later, baby."

Daisy lingered for a moment, her mouth partially open as if she wanted to say something. She swallowed and then said, "Have fun. I'll be thinking of you."

Elias remained in the carpark until Daisy's backlights vanished in the dark. It didn't surprise him she was jealous of not attending tonight, partially because she wouldn't meet Teddy and, partially because he would be with Ava unsupervised. Her childishness angered him because if she couldn't trust him, what else did they have?

He entered the hotel lobby. Other guests pooled in the reception area, elaborately and purposely dressed in the colours of the fundraiser—black and gold. They glittered under the chandeliers dangling from the ceiling. A cherry-red Mercedes—the grand prize of the raffle—was stationed in the centre of the room cordoned off by velvet rope. Elias had spent two weeks persuading the local dealership owner to donate the car for a good cause. Flashing his ticket at the door, he walked into the grandly lit ballroom, adorned with golden banners and balloons. A band belted out a popular pop song on the stage that stretched the length of the ballroom, built for the occasion. Round tables filled the room, already occupied by excited guests sipping on beer and champagne.

Elias spotted Ava in the centre of the room, corralled by a group of businessmen. She was dressed in a figure-hugging teal gown and black high heels, her fiery red hair pinned back neatly. A diamond necklace dripped around her neck. She looked exquisite. As he drew closer, he could see why Ava had drawn the crowd. Teddy Rollins was attached to her arm. He embodied the idyllic Hollywood movie star—tall and brooding, mouthful of perfect, white teeth, strong jawline, and honey-coloured hair. He was better looking in the flesh, seducing everyone around him with a flashing smile.

Elias contemplated either speaking to the MC waiting for him backstage or introducing himself to the movie star. It seemed Ava made the decision for him, spotting him through the crowd.

"Elias! Oh, there you are," she called out, shooting her hand in the air. "Come over here and meet our very generous host committee."

He plastered on a friendly smile and sidled up to Ava. She slipped her arm across his shoulders and introduced him to the wealthy business owners, donors and of course, Teddy who donated thousands of dollars towards the fundraiser.

"Nice to meet you, mate," Teddy said, shaking Elias's hand firmly. "Ava's told me a lot about you." His smile was blinding, and Elias averted his gaze to the man's lingering hand on Ava's lower back. They were practically glued to the hip.

"You too. Congratulations on the Best Actor Oscar win," he replied. "I'm sure it's a great honour."

"It definitely strokes your ego, mate," Teddy said with a laugh. "The film industry is full of people ready to make you feel like the big man. Nothing can beat that feeling of superiority."

"Teddy keeps his Oscar locked in a cabinet in his bedroom," Ava intervened, glancing at the bewitched committee around her. "I've seen it before. It's not as big as it looks on television."

"Not what you wanna hear from a woman, am I right, gents?" Teddy threw his head back and laughed. Like a pack of hyenas, the circle joined him in the joke. "I need a drink," he announced. "I heard the Pameer Hotel has a spectacular Shiraz." He dropped his arm from Ava's waist and sauntered off towards the bar, followed by his little cohort of admirers.

"He's exactly what I pictured him to be like," Elias mused as he watched Teddy slip onto a bar stool. "Quite the charmer." It didn't take long for the actor to be completely surrounded by young, beautiful women.

"Yes, he is. Even worse in bed," Ava responded. Her eyes glistened with mischief when Elias's jaw dropped open. "Oh, come on, Elias. I'm only playing." She squeezed his arm. "You're so uptight all the time. You need to loosen up, honey." She plucked two glasses of champagne from a waiter walking by and handed a flute to Elias.

"Toast with me. Tonight, we mark a new era for the company. In the first hour, we've raised fifty thousand dollars and people are still sober! When the prizes were wheeled onto stage, they went crazy. The Tiffany necklace has been drawn, so has the Paris holiday." She glanced behind her to the wrapped boxes of prizes on the stage, under the watchful eye of a security guard. Smart phones, jewellery, designer hand bags, cameras, and tablets had been donated by local businesses and industry leaders.

"Did you end up increasing the ticket price for the car?" Elias asked. "Liam told me you were discussing it."

"Yes, I've raised it to five thousand dollars," Ava replied proudly. "It's pocket money for these people. The rich love raffles and it's going to a good cause." She took a sip of her champagne, her emerald gaze lingering over the glass rim. "You've done well, Elias. I'm amazed at what you've managed to do in a short time. Some of these people are the most wealthiest and influential in Sydney. Well done."

"It was a joint effort." Liam materialised beside Ava dressed in a black designer suit and polished dress shoes. His dark hair was brushed off his wide forehead in a sideways part, making him look even more like a secret agent.

"Liam, when did you get here?"

"Thirty minutes ago. Been at the bar drinking away my sobriety."

Elias watched Ava's shoulders stiffen as Liam leaned in to kiss her cheek. Her gaze snapped to his, almost begging, an unspoken plea to intervene. Liam's arm found its way around her waist, pinning her to him.

"Would you like another drink, Liam?" Elias asked, jerking his thumb towards the bar. "I was going to get a beer and sit at our table before the show starts. Ava's busy greeting the guests anyway, so why don't you join me?"

Liam glanced at Ava with uncertainty. "Are you sure you can handle everyone by yourself? I have the list of guests in my head. I know who's coming and who's not."

"No, I can manage by myself, Liam," Ava replied, slipping from his touch. "Go have a beer with Elias. I've got the rounds to do." Practically pushing him away, Ava was momentarily distracted when the prime minister and his wife entered the room. Before she left to greet them, Ava flashed Elias an indistinct—yet grateful—smile.

~ ~ ~

Elias downed his sixth shot of whiskey for the night and grimaced as the alcohol burned down his throat. Rarely a big drinker, he greedily accepted every glass placed in front of him, so it didn't take long for the floor to start spinning.

Liam sat beside him, his chin perched in one hand, eyelids heavy with intoxication. Empty beer bottles filled the space in front of him. Stationed in his chair for the past hour, he'd kept an eagle eye on Ava as she laughed, drank, and ate with guests. Any time Elias spotted her through the crowd, she had a wineglass in her hand, given to her by an admirer. In her skin-tight, curve-enhancing gown, she'd inadvertently become the star of the evening, like a bride on her wedding day. All eyes were on her.

Elias dug his mobile from his pocket and re-read the two text messages Daisy had sent him earlier in the night. He hadn't bothered to reply, not in the mood to talk to her. He couldn't bring himself to reward Daisy for her jealousy. He knew Ava cast a long shadow in their relationship but Elias was a loyal, one-woman kind of man. Always would be.

"You're brooding, mate."

"Huh?" Elias's gaze snapped to Liam.

A fresh, perspiring beer hung inches from his lips, given to him by a waiter doing the rounds. "You look pissed about something," he added before taking a swig.

Elias shook his head, reaching for his own drink. "I'm not pissed."

"Come on, I know the look. Daisy's angry at you because you didn't bring her tonight. Is that right?"

Ava sauntered across Elias's line of sight and she threw him another one of her subtle smirks. It was small, but still there. It gave him the confidence and reassurance he needed to slip his phone back into his pocket and enjoy the night. "Daisy wanted to know when I'm coming home."

Liam leaned across the table drunkenly and pointed a wobbly finger at him. "You're an honest man so you would never make the first move. But what would you do if she did?"

"What are you talking about?"

Liam jerked his chin in Ava's direction. "They don't call her a man-eater for nothing. She will chew you up and spit you out."

Defiantly, Elias crossed his arms over his chest. "Never going to happen."

"Ha! There is so much sexual tension between you two I can practically cut it with a knife."

"You're drunk, Liam." Elias yanked the beer out of the man's hand. "Why do I have to keep telling people my relationship with Ava is purely professional? I will never go there, nor will she."

"You keep telling yourself that, mate. I was married to the woman for six years. Not even a wedding ring stopped her." Liam scowled, his eyes narrowing as he stared hard across the room. "Once you get a few drinks into 'er, she will do anything—or anyone."

Elias blew out a burst of hot air and mumbled, "Maybe I should've stayed home."

"Nah, you're my drinking buddy. Are you staying at the hotel tonight or catching the train home?"

Elias had considered going home and confronting Daisy, but cruelly decided she should think of him being in the company of a drunken Ava Wolfe. "I'm staying on the fifth floor. It's just me and the bed tonight. Alone."

The big screen above the stage displayed a live counter of money being donated, clicking over to one hundred thousand dollars when Elias ordered another shot. Populating the ballroom, the guests drank port from crystal glasses, ate caviar and lobster, and enjoyed showing off their raffle wins to their friends. A lot of money had gone into keeping the rich happy for one night and Elias hoped Blue Tail's generosity would ripple across elite society. The company needed it. Ava needed it.

He studied her as she stood by the bar, encircled by a ring of tipsy businessmen. He was sober enough to see she was enjoying the male attention—purring like a kitten as the men piled more free drinks into her. Her gaze flicked upwards and fixed with his. Something flashed in her eyes and it was enough for Elias to get out of his chair and walk towards the bar.

The ring broke when he approached, completely shattering when he forced his place next to Ava, slipping the sherry from her fingers. "I think you've had enough," he said. "The Mercedes's about to be drawn. You're the one drawing the ticket, remember?"

"You can do that," she replied, curling her arm around his shoulders, her warm breath tickling his cheek. "Everyone in this room paid handsomely to see some hottie give away the car. The model I hired pulled out at the last minute and you're the hottest guy here. You do it."

Elias bit his tongue. Ava was drunker than he thought. He steered her through the crowd and pulled out a chair for her at their table. Liam was gone, leaving behind an array of empty beer bottles in his wake. "Have you eaten tonight?" Elias asked, pushing a plate of cheese and crackers towards Ava. "I've only seen you drink."

"I was mingling," she argued. "The room is full of potential advertisers. I haven't seen you do any socializing."

"That's your forte," he retorted, preparing a cracker for himself. As he ate, the MC appeared by the left wing of the stage and waved him over. Elias turned to Ava. "I'll be back soon."

"Where are you going?"

"Just stay here. Don't accept any more drinks." He walked through the crowds and met with the MC hanging back in the shadows. "Is everything all right?"

"Ms. Wolfe's due on stage in ten minutes," the MC exclaimed, his round cheeks flushed red. "We're drawing the ticket for the car and we need to get her prepped."

Behind the curtains, Elias could see the curvaceous silhouette of the Mercedes as it waited off stage, driven in from the foyer. "Pop the mic pack on me. I'm going up instead of Ava."

"What? You're not on the itinerary."

"Things change, just like business. These people will understand. They came here for the car, anyway." Elias pointed in the direction of the crew running around backstage. "Who do I speak to for the mic setup?"

Chapter 9

Twelve minutes past midnight, Elias half-carried, half-dragged a drunk Ava to the fifth floor of the hotel. With the night's excitement still ringing in his ears, he paused outside her room, propping Ava against the wall as he searched her clutch purse for the key.

"You did good tonight," she drawled, a hapless smile plastered across her face. "I'm proud of you. We'll be in the papers tomorrow for all the right reasons."

After Elias pulled the winning raffle ticket and stood with the victor for photographs, he returned to the crowd, finding Ava sitting alone at the bar, running her finger up and down an empty wineglass. He found the act incredibly sexy, like a cat twitching its tail in pique. She had sobered up enough to throw him a look heavy with drunk lust. He had ignored it because when Ava drank, her guard was lowered, disarming her. Breakable. Weak. He didn't want to become that type of man.

Now, as he tipped her clutch's contents onto the carpet, he wondered if she would remember tonight's events in the morning. He pushed aside her mobile phone, a driver's license, a tampon, and a candy wrapper before locating the slim white card. Triumphantly, he swiped it and grinned when the door unlocked. He helped her inside, using his elbow to turn on the light switch.

"Why are you so nice to me?" Ava mumbled as they wandered to the couch. Elias assumed it was safer here than trying to get her into bed.

He lowered her down onto the plush cushions. "You're my friend. I care about you," he replied matter-of-factly, sliding one heel off her foot. "Anyone would do the same."

"No, they wouldn't." She raked her hand over her face, her lips twisting with self-loathing. "I'm a bitch. Everyone knows that. I have no friends outside of work."

"You have me." Elias placed both heels on the floor beside the couch and leaned down to sweep a lock of hair from her face. "You're a talented, savvy, and beautiful woman. I've learned more in the months with you than I ever did at university."

"Why are people so frightened of me? My staff practically cower when I walk past them."

"They don't know you, Ava. People are scared of the unknown. You rebuilt Blue Tail Media from the ashes and that's a hard thing to do. You had to be tough and resilient to survive." His hand lingered on her cheek, his thumb caressing her smooth, white skin. He felt his phone vibrate in his pocket, knowing it was Daisy checking up on him again. A part of him wanted to walk out the door and go home to her, but he didn't want to leave Ava. He felt responsible for her, to ensure she didn't hurt herself—or anyone else from hurting her. Her eyes closed when his thumb brushed her parted lips.

"Are you sure you're okay?" he asked.

Ava sat up slowly, taking his arm for support. "I'm drunker than I thought I was." Her jade gaze locked with his. "You don't have to stay with me. I'm fine." Her hands reached behind her neck and she unclasped the necklace. Holding a pool of diamonds in one hand, she added, "Go home to Daisy. I can hear your phone vibrating in your pocket."

Elias swallowed the lump in his throat. "I don't know if I want to."

Ava shuffled over and patted the space next to her. "Sit down then. Let's talk. I would offer you a drink but I think this hotel is fresh out of alcohol after the fundraiser."

Elias laughed. "How about something to eat? We can charge the company room service."

A wicked smile crossed Ava's face. "How devilish of you, Elias. I'm all right for now. Go home to Daisy. I'm pretty sure I'm in her bad books for keeping you away tonight."

As they sat shoulder to shoulder, Elias felt every move Ava made, every breath she took, every nerve synapse inside her body. He was sure she could feel his too because she turned and looked at him, clarity in her eyes.

"You don't want to go home," she said.

Elias pulled at a loose thread on the couch, begging for his heart to slow down. Maybe it was the alcohol in his gut, or the adrenalin still coursing through his veins, but all he wanted to do was take Ava to bed and clear her from his system. Liam was right. The sexual tension between them was palpable. It was so strong he could almost smell it, radiating off their bodies like smoke.

"I don't think I'm ready to face all of that yet," he whispered, snapping his gaze to her large, wide eyes and mouth that begged to be kissed.

"Face what?"

"What I'm about to do." He was upon her so fast, she gasped, capturing Ava's face in his hands. He kissed her. Hard. Like his life depended on it.

~ ~ ~

Ava drew a sharp intake of breath as Elias's azure eyes—now dark with ravenous hunger—pinned her to the couch. A heat bellowed off him in waves, something she recognised as raw, unbreakable desire. He wanted her.

When he spoke, she listened, absorbing every word he said, feeling insecure when his eyes toured her face. Then, his lips crashed upon hers, so fast she missed a breath. His hands felt cool against her cheeks, despite the heat in the room. He tasted so sweet and warm.

Elias groaned deep in his throat when she kissed him back. Ava knew it was wrong to reciprocate, but judging by the desperation in Elias's kisses, he wasn't thinking of his girlfriend anymore.

His fingers buried into her hair, pulling it from the jade hair clip holding it together. His kiss was deep and passionate, leaving Ava breathless. She wanted more. She climbed onto his lap, straddling his slim hips, pressing herself into his erection. Elias moaned, shifting his hands from her hair to the hem of her dress, lifting it up to squeeze her bottom. Pleasure ribboned through Ava as his nails bit into her flesh, inciting bittersweet pain.

Her fingers fumbled to unbutton his shirt, frantic to see him underneath his clothes. Elias appeared to have the same idea, locating the zipper on her dress, unfastening it, freeing her from the confines of the fabric. He pulled the straps down over her shoulders, feathering hot kisses along her collarbone. Ava tilted her back and let out the breath she'd been holding in. Like her, it was if a dam inside Elias had broken, freeing all the tension inside her.

With both hands, Elias jerked the dress's neckline down until her breasts sprung free, aching for his touch. Taking one hot peak into his mouth, he sucked and licked, earning a moan from her lips. Ava tore at his shirt, almost ripping it from his body.

"I want you," she breathed, her hands reaching for his zipper. When she wrapped her fingers around him, he gasped. Ava silenced him with a kiss, pushing down the guilt inside her. Her past actions had destroyed relationships before, ending her young marriage to Liam. But Elias was a good man. He didn't deserve to lose Daisy if their actions got them into trouble. Ava was just lonely and there were plenty of faceless men downstairs more than willing to share her bed tonight. She broke the kiss, preparing to let Elias down softly when he stood from the couch, taking her with him.

He heaved her into his arms, carrying her to the bedroom down the hall. He kicked the door open and tossed her onto the mattress, stripping off her gown and underwear without a word. She lay naked in front of him, unabashed, watching him undress.

His body was lean and toned, with a sculptured chest and arms. A birthmark shaped like a starfish imprinted the skin on his left hip.

When he removed his pants, she inhaled sharply, not at the sight of him, but at the conflicting feelings inside her. She was doing it again, diving down the rabbit hole, but this time she knew of the consequences.

Her face twisted in pleasure when he slipped inside her, hooking her legs around his waist. When they found a rhythm, she welcomed the touches, smells, and tingles Elias incited on her body. His fingers left a scorched trail in their wake, burning her skin, making her wanting more. He pumped into her so fast and quick that he hurt her, but Ava didn't tell him to stop. She liked it rough.

"I don't have a . . ." Elias finally spoke, breathless in the nook of her neck. His entire body shuddered and she knew he was close.

"I'm on the pill," she whispered back, lifting her hips against his belly, wanting him to go deeper. "Keep going."

As they climaxed together, Ava fell back into the pillow, out of breath, sore, and completely satisfied. She was certain it was the copious amounts of alcohol she consumed tonight that made sex with Elias the best of her life, but he fed the urge inside her, making her feel wanted and attractive.

Not one for chatting after making love, Ava rolled over to check her mobile on the nightstand. There was a text from the MC congratulating her on the successful night and a barrage of drunk dialings from Liam.

As she climbed out of bed, eager for a shower and one last glass of wine, Ava turned and studied Elias sleeping among the tangled sheets. She would think fondly of tonight, of the unspoken pleasures Elias unearthed inside her, even if it was a one-off fling. He would return to his normal life in the morning and she would go back to the office, like nothing ever happened.

Chapter 10

Elias awoke with a start. A beam of sunlight broke into the bedroom, blinding him when he rolled over. Ava slept with her back to him, naked, her fiery, red hair fanned across the silk pillow. Her milky, white skin begged to be touched, but a crashing wave of guilt overcame him, forcing him out of bed. The sheets still reeked of sex. His discarded clothes lay scattered across the floor. He had cheated on Daisy. The line he didn't want to cross was now blurred.

Elias wandered into the bathroom and closed the door. He couldn't look at Ava now, too ashamed to see last night's indiscretion painted on the sheets. He took a shower and dressed, grabbing his shoes and jacket on the way out. He didn't bother to leave a note or text Ava that he was going. What happened last night was a mistake, a one-time thing. He was drunk. She was drunk. He had to move on and put it behind him.

He caught a train back to his apartment, knowing Daisy had stayed overnight. As he walked down the hallway, he wondered if she could tell by looking at him that he had slept with another woman. Did he look different to others? He certainly felt different.

He unlocked the front door and stepped inside. The television was on, broadcasting an episode of *Day Break*. The rich aroma of coffee filled the air, soothing his nerves.

"Daisy, I'm back."

She materialised from his bedroom, dressed in an oversized T-shirt. It looked like she hadn't slept one wink. Dark bags shadowed her eyes and her blonde hair was pulled back into a messy bun. Yesterday's makeup was smeared across her face.

"Hey, baby," he purred, tossing his jacket over a kitchen barstool. He opened his arms wide, expecting a welcoming hug. Instead, she greeted him with a nasty slap across his face.

"Ow! What the fuck was that for?"

"You ignored my texts last night," Daisy shot back. "I was worried, Elias."

"What texts? Do you mean the fifteen messages you sent me throughout the night? I couldn't answer every single one. I was working, Daisy."

Her lips pursed together with hurt. "If you had invited me, I wouldn't have blown your phone up with texts."

"I've told you it was an employee-only event. You're being melodramatic."

"I saw you check-in on Facebook and comment on a few people's statuses, so you were using your phone." She perched her hands on her hips. "Why did you ignore me?"

"I'm telling you why! I was waist-deep entertaining Sydney's elite society. I didn't have time to stop. I was there to make sure they drunk the bar dry and donated their dusty, old money." Elias pinched the bridge of his nose and drew a calming breath. "Look, I'm sorry I didn't reply to your messages. Let me take you out for breakfast. A new vegan café opened up in Bondi. I think you'll like it. They serve sugar-, dairy-, and cruelty-free food."

Daisy's eyes surveyed his crumpled white shirt and he prayed Ava hadn't left any lipstick marks. "Have you showered already?"

"I did at the hotel."

She reached over and flicked some dried food off his collar. "I'll get this washed and ironed so you can wear it tomorrow. It's your good work shirt."

"So, do you want to check out that new café? I need a good damn coffee."

A small smirk appeared on Daisy's lips. "Only if you're driving. Parking in Bondi is a bitch."

~ ~ ~

The twenty-minute drive into Bondi was silent and awkward, a wedge building between them. There was something odd about Elias. Daisy could sense it as she watched him across the café table. He spoke differently, held himself differently and even touched her differently. A million excuses ran through her mind as she tried to make sense of it. Maybe he was just tired from the fundraiser or angry at her for bombarding him with texts. Either way, Elias wasn't the same man she said goodbye to last night at the hotel.

Did something happen at the event? She pushed down the unease in her gut and reached for her soy coffee.

"You haven't told me anything about the fundraiser," she said, taking a sip, pushing the last sugar-free chocolate cookie towards him. "I'm dying to hear about it. Who was there?"

Eager to see if Elias would take her peace offering, Daisy curled her fingers around her cup and waited. Something flickered in his dark eyes—a memory, perhaps—and he leaned back in his chair.

"It was a good night," he said at last. "Heaps of money was donated to the charity and people seemed to enjoy the food and prizes. An eighty-thousand-dollar Mercedes was raffled off to a rich guy who would probably never drive it."

"What colour was it?"

"Cherry red."

The next sentence slipped out before she could stop herself. "What did Ava wear?"

Elias's shoulders instantly tensed and she knew she'd hit a nerve. "I'm going to get another coffee." He stood up and pinched the Sunday paper off another table. "Check the society section in here. There may be a photo of Ava's dress." He sauntered off towards the register.

Obediently, Daisy flipped through the newspaper to the society page and found an article on the fundraiser. She skimmed through it, looking for Ava's name and any gossip on the woman. The piece had a three-page spread, mostly filled with photographs of the night. Happy and drunk business people stared back at her. There was one photo that didn't match the others, a private moment shared between two people. As Daisy inspected the image more closely, a cold sweat broke across her skin. It was Elias and Ava captured in deep conversation. They weren't touching but Daisy could see the intimacy between them, as they leaned toward each other, their bodies facing.

She lowered the paper and studied Elias walking back to their table, his hands thrust deep into his pockets, his head casually cocked to the side. Women eyed him hungrily over their sunglasses as he strode past them. He was a handsome man, someone you expected to see on the cover of *GQ* or *Vogue*. He had model-good looks and a body of an athlete.

Daisy couldn't deny she felt threatened when Elias accepted the job at Blue Tail Media. The rumours surrounding Ava Wolfe and her alleged affairs could fill a novel. But Elias was a loyal and loving boyfriend. He would never be seduced by Ava's charms. *Surely*.

He sat back down, jerking his chin towards the article in front of her. "Is that a spread on the fundraiser? I haven't seen any press on it yet."

Wordlessly, she pushed the paper towards him, studying his face for any emotion or reaction as he read. There was nothing. Deadpan.

"Did you find out what Ava was wearing?" he asked. "I have no idea about fashion or designers."

She pointed to a full-length photograph of Ava draped over another guest and bit down her jealousy. The woman looked radiant as usual, the knee-length dress accentuating her famous figure. The diamonds around her neck were blinding. "It's a Gerald Loft gown," she explained. "His designs are popular for their feminine silhouette and vibrant colours. I saw Ava's dress in last month's *Vogue*. Must've cost a fortune."

"Does this guy have a store in Sydney?"

"Probably. Why?"

Elias reached over the table and caressed her cheek, his eyes softening. "Let me buy you something nice. You deserve it."

For a split second, Daisy thought she saw something else in his blue eyes other than affection. Guilt? Remorse? She couldn't tell, but it made her feel sick in the pit of her stomach. She swallowed the lump in her throat and forced a smile. "I think there's a store in the city. Can we go?"

"Sure."

"Do you have to work?"

"Today? It's Sunday, Daisy."

"I remember your phone didn't stop ringing last weekend."

Elias fished his phone out of his pocket and turned it off. "Look, my mobile is off. No calls from anyone. It's just you and me today."

After they paid for breakfast and walked along the shore of Bondi beach, hand in hand, Daisy wondered if she'd lost a part of Elias. He'd been drifting away ever since he started working for Ava. It chilled her to the bone at the thought because she wasn't willing to share him with anyone, no matter who the bitch was. Elias possessed her entire heart, body, and soul. And always would.

Chapter 11

The office was empty when Elias stepped off the lift on Monday morning. Carrying a cappuccino in one hand and his briefcase in the other, he navigated through the quiet floor to his shared office with Ava.

She wasn't in yet so he took the moment of solitude to turn on his computer, sort through unread emails, and attempt to wipe the memories of Saturday night from his mind. Images of Ava's milk-white body writhing underneath him replayed like a movie, haunting him whenever he closed his eyes.

For two days, the guilt had chipped away at his resolve, pushing him to come clean to Daisy. But he feared her suspicions were already aroused. After breakfast, they strolled Bondi beach where she interrogated him further about the fundraiser, asking what he did, where he sat, who he danced with. Elias deserved it. He'd cheated on the one woman who supported and loved him no matter what.

The office door opened, and Ava strutted into the room, handbag hooked over her arm, eyes shaded by designer sunglasses. "Good morning," she said, dumping her empty takeaway coffee cup in the bin. She slid her glasses down her nose and tossed him a smile. "How was the rest of your weekend?"

"Ava, we need to talk."

She dropped her purse onto her desk and let out a sigh. "I'm not two feet inside the office and you're already brooding. What's wrong? You're not worried out about Saturday night, are you?"

"Daisy suspects we slept together," Elias blurted.

"What?" Ava removed her sunglasses and tossed them onto her desk. "I was talking about the prime minister getting plastered in front of the photographers. He's going to regret that behaviour when the photos come out." She switched on her PC, her gaze fixed on him. "Did you tell Daisy about us?"

"Of course not."

"How do you know she's suspicious?"

Elias drained the remains of his lukewarm coffee—wishing he had something stronger—and approached her desk, towering over her. "I've known this woman since we were teenagers. I can read her like a book. She knows. I can't keep lying to her."

Ava's eyes shadowed with hurt. "Are you ashamed of what happened between us? We were drunk."

"And that makes it okay? I'm sorry, Ava. Saturday night was a mistake. I never should've allowed my feelings to get in the way of our relationship." He swallowed the lump in his throat, fearing what he was going to say next. His life could change in a heartbeat. "I think it's best I resign before the shit hits the fan."

The colour returned to Ava's cheeks and she stood up to match him, a vicious fire burning behind her green eyes. "I'm not going to accept that, Elias. From what I recall, you were the one who instigated the first move. You couldn't keep your hands off me!"

"Ava, I didn't know what I was—"

A knock sounded at the door, silencing them both. Blake Parker popped his head into the room tentatively as if he'd heard their entire conversation. "Ava, I'm sorry to interrupt. We're waiting for you in the boardroom. The editorial meeting's about to start."

Ava pursed her lips into a thin line. "I thought the meeting started at nine-thirty. I'm in the middle of something here. Can you wait ten more minutes?"

Blake's eyes snapped towards Elias and back at Ava. "I guess we can. Will Elias be joining us?"

"No, he's got calls to make this morning. We've been inundated with emails and calls from people who attended the fundraiser. I want Elias to mend fences with the press too. Everyone needs to know Blue Tail is moving on from the scandal."

Elias remained in his seat, watching Ava gather her tablet before leaving with Blake. She tossed him a glance over her shoulder as she closed the door. He wanted to reach an understanding about Saturday night. He didn't want to spend all day on the phone or kissing the asses of newspaper editors. He'd already betrayed Daisy and the guilt weighed heavily on his shoulders. Quitting his job seemed like the logical thing to do. He had gained enough experience at Blue Tail to find a similar role elsewhere. But he couldn't justify leaving the company yet. He had only seen the tip of the iceberg. The scandal was still fresh on people's minds and he had heaps of publicity and event ideas to tackle the lingering stigma. Above all, he felt indebted to Ava. She had given him what he craved most: a fulfilling and rewarding career.

As Elias turned his computer on and scrolled through his unread emails, it terrified him to think that it wasn't the company he was prepared to part with. It was Ava. Their one night of passion might've been a mistake, but he couldn't get it out of his head, imprinted on his memory like a tattoo— the yearning in Ava's eyes, the hunger in her kisses, her heart pounding against his chest.

He was determined to keep those memories buried and the harsh reality that went with them. If Daisy ever found out, she would leave him. But worst of all, if her father got involved, Elias had little chance of seeing the next sunrise.

~ ~ ~

A soft breeze carried the crisp aroma of saltwater air, filling the beach-side café. It was busy for Saturday morning, with surfers, joggers and couples spilling onto the veranda, drinking coffee and eating breakfast. The laid-back atmosphere was stimulating, unparalleled to Sydney's bustling orchestra of car horns, loud music, and industry.

"Do you want another coffee, honey?" Karen asked, nibbling on the remains of her chocolate chip cookie. "I can go for another one."

"I'm fine, Mum," Elias replied as he sipped his lukewarm cappuccino. "I'm still going with this one. I don't think I can have another cup."

"If you're not having one, I won't either." Karen pushed her empty plate aside so she could lean on the table. "So tell me more about your new job. You haven't told me anything since your first week. I get all my gossip from the magazines. Are you still enjoying it?"

After a big week of fighting his conflicting emotions, Elias decided some time away might ease the tightness in his chest. On Friday night, he drove up the coast to spend the weekend with his mother. A part of him felt bad for leaving everything behind—his girlfriend, unresolved issues with Ava, and his work phone—but his mental health was dependent on this respite.

Elias tore at his napkin underneath the table. "It's hard work and I'm rarely home before seven most nights, but I'm enjoying it." He tossed his mother a wayward smile. "I wanted a challenging job and I got one."

A spot above Karen's manicured eyebrow ticked. "I hope you don't work too hard, honey," she said, patting his arm. "I worry about your health. You work too hard. You burned out in your last job, remember? Does Ava Wolfe treat you well? I've read many things about her in the papers."

Elias tried to hide the involuntary blush in his cheeks. "Ava's very good to me. I get paid for any overtime and

I'm the only one in the office who gets ninety-minute lunch breaks. But in return, I'm on call twenty-four/seven and must have my work phone on me at all times. Whatever Ava needs, Ava gets."

"She sounds high maintenance," Karen said. "Do you enjoy working for her?"

"She's not a bad person. The media portrays her as this ruthless, man-eating bombshell. She's nothing like that. She's a hardworking businesswoman trying to keep her multimillion-dollar company afloat."

Karen's lips thinned. "Please see your situation from my point of view. You're my only child and I want the best for you. The last thing I want is for you to be exploited or taken advantage of. It happened quite a bit when you were younger."

"Do you mean the fish and chip shop owned by the bikies? Okay, working long hours without pay was a mistake," Elias said, "but I had to learn things the hard way. I'm a grown man, Mum, and I don't regret making the decision leaving the studio. I was bored doing the same thing every day. At least with Blue Tail, I'm meeting new people and building my career."

"What does Daisy think of your job?" Karen questioned. "Before you resigned from the studio, you were thinking about getting back together. I want grandchildren before I'm eighty, Elias."

As much as Elias wanted to bury the memories of his night with Ava, he realised he was never going to be free of them. Every time he looked at Daisy, he saw Ava's face twisting in pleasure. He couldn't even touch her without recalling the soft curves of Ava's milky white skin. Unwillingly, he had welcomed Ava into his soul.

"I'm working on my relationship with Daisy right now," he said. "The long hours apart are making it hard, but I'm willing to make it work. She doesn't understand what I do so it's difficult to explain why I call clients at one a.m. or duck out at midnight to pick up a report."

"Do you love her?"

Elias hesitated for a second and inwardly hated himself for it. "Yes, I do."

"Oh, Elias." The disapproval in Karen's voice raked across his skin. "I can read you like a book, my boy." She reached across the table and squeezed his hands. "It's cruel to lead someone on, especially when it comes to love. You need to spend some time to think if this relationship is really going to work. If you love Daisy, you need to make a sacrifice somewhere else. Come home when she expects you and go on a holiday together. If you think it's hard work now, just wait until you're married."

Elias tossed back his cold coffee and welcomed the bitter, milky taste. He didn't know what he wanted anymore. Leaving Sydney for the weekend meant he left his emotions behind, but they always followed him, like his guilt.

"Mr. Elias Dorne?" A man materialised by Elias's shoulder, casting a shadow across the table. "May I speak with you for a minute?"

Elias glanced up and noticed the notepad and mobile in the stranger's hands. "Who's asking?"

"I'm Mike Corden from *The Coastal Times*. Do you mind if I ask you a few questions?"

Elias shot his mother a quick glance. "I'm off-duty today, mate. I'm with my mother. Call the office on Monday and I'll speak to you then."

Mike cleared his throat and tucked his notepad into his jeans pocket. "Look, my editor's been riding my ass about coming up with a good piece and I can't go back to him empty handed. I want to hear more about Blue Tail Media and its climb back to the top." He grinned widely. "It will make for a great profile piece. My readership covers all of the coast."

"Where did you say you were from again?"

"*Coastal Times.*"

Elias let out a sigh. "Maybe some other time."

Karen turned in her seat and patted Mike's arm. "It's okay, honey. You can take my chair."

"Mum?"

She pushed her chair back and stood up, slipping her sunglasses on. "It's fine, Elias. I'll leave you boys to it. I'll meet you outside the ice cream shop in half an hour."

Elias watched his mother retreat down the road as the journalist took her seat. She owed him big time for this.

"I promise I won't be long," Mike said excitedly, placing his mobile on the table between them. "I appreciate you taking the time for me."

"I didn't have much of a choice," Elias replied dryly.

"Your mother is a wonderful woman," Mike preened, ordering himself a coffee as a waiter appeared with a menu. "I can only imagine you've inherited a lot of her charming traits."

"Please start this interview," Elias pressed, growing incredibly frustrated. "I would like to get back to her."

"Of course. Do you mind if I record this conversation?"

"No."

Mike pressed a button on his phone. "This is Mike Corden with *The Coastal Times* sitting with Elias Dorne of Blue Tail Media." He flipped open his notepad, his pen hovering above the paper. "Mr. Dorne, I would like to start with your previous position at disgraced television show Manny Magpie. You resigned shortly after the studio was outed in the scandal involving the presenter. Was it your intention abandoning the studio when it needed you?"

"I never abandoned it," Elias insisted. "I was there from the day they aired their first program. Bill Gander gave me a chance when no one else would. I supported the company during the incident and moved on when I was satisfied I had done all that I could. I'm not the type of man to turn my back on the people who helped build my career."

"Speaking of that, I've been hearing your name pop up in certain circles. In such a short time, you've created a solid career in the industry. It's quite impressive. Can you describe your job title at Blue Tail?"

Elias cleared his throat and leaned towards the phone. "I'm the Director of Communications. My role involves event management, content control, sales and public relations."

"Were you employed when the Bobbie Hayes scandal hit the papers?"

"No, I was hired afterwards."

"Doing what?"

"What I said before."

Mike's lips twitched before he scribbled on his notepad. "Blue Tail Media's reputation was very rocky after the scandal. The company's stocks plummeted and its portfolio halved. Ava Wolfe was appointed CEO after extensive years in business. Do you think she's succeeded at rebuilding Blue Tail's public image?"

Elias swallowed the lump in his throat. "Ms. Wolfe is a strategic businesswoman. She understands the market and its fluctuations, and after owning businesses in the past, she recognises consumer strengths. She handled the scandal very graciously."

Elias saw his mother round the corner and shot her an unspoken plea to rescue him from the intrusive journalist. Instead, she flashed him a smile, waved, and stepped into a gift shop.

Mike didn't seem to notice, asking another question. "*The Daily News* said that last weekend's charity fundraiser was a brazen move for popularity. Why do you think it defied the critics and became a newsworthy success?"

"The company has loyal shareholders," Elias replied.

"We provided a quality night with good food and good entertainment. People respond well to charity."

"What's your background, Elias?" Mike pressed, with a brief smile. "Tell me more about you. Are you single, married, have children?"

Elias rarely did interviews for this reason. He understood human interest stories sold newspapers, but he was a businessman, not a celebrity, and he wanted this chance to promote the company instead. No personal crap. "I would prefer not to say, Mike. I doubt your readers would care about my childhood."

"You'll be surprised, Elias. My readership may be purely business but they are people too." He leaned forward in his chair. "Look, I promise I won't ask about your first kiss or job, I just want to know more about your family, especially your lovely mother."

Elias sighed. "Fine, I'll comply but not everything I say is to be published. My family life is private. Got it?"

Mike gave him a curt nod. "You have my word." He cleared his throat and consulted his notepad. "Okay, let's continue."

As Elias described his sibling-free, nomadic, and chilled childhood to the enthused journalist, Karen made her way back to the café, carrying multiple shopping bags in her hands. She pulled out a chair beside Mike and listened intently as he threw questions at Elias about the origin of his passion for media. They'd been sitting for an hour when Mike asked one question that sent a cold rush through Elias's body.

"What's your relationship with Ava Wolfe?"

"What-what do you mean?" He hoped the quiver in his voice wasn't noticeable.

"I saw the pictures of the fundraiser. You and Ava looked pretty close."

"We have a strictly—"

"Elias has always been a ladies' man," Karen interjected proudly, squeezing his arm. "I'm not surprised women are attracted to him. Even as a child, those big, blue eyes got a lot of attention from females."

"Mum!" Elias exclaimed. "This is a business meeting, not a celebrity interview."

"It can be," Mike said with a smile. "Now, answer my question. What's your relationship with Ms. Wolfe? She has quite a reputation in the industry for her—"

"All right, I've had enough," Elias interjected, slamming his fist on the table. "Mike, I'm assuming you have everything you want?"

"I do for now." A disappointed frown pulled at his lips. "Do you have a business card if I need to clarify things?"

Elias removed a card from his wallet, slapping it onto the table. "Call me during office hours. *Only* office hours."

Mike gathered his things and shot out his hand. "It was nice meeting you, Elias. I'll email you a copy of the article when it's published."

"When will that be?"

Mike hooked his canvas bag over his shoulder. "Next week sometime. We go to print this afternoon." He turned to Karen and shook her hand. "It was lovely meeting you, Mrs. Dorne. I appreciate you giving up your breakfast so I can interview your son."

Karen let out a girlish giggle. "My pleasure. Anytime."

Elias bit back a groan and slipped into his jacket hanging on the back of his chair. "Come on, Mum. We've got a movie to catch." He turned to Mike. "We'll be in touch."

"I look forward to it." Then Mike leaned in, squeezed Elias's shoulder, and whispered, "You're fucking brilliant, you know that?"

"I'm what?"

"Hooking up with the boss. It's done wonders to your career."

"You've got it all wrong, Mike. I'm not sleeping with Ava."

A knowing sneer pulled at the journalist's lips. "You can play dumb all you want, Elias. I have photographic evidence. There are more than a few staff at Pameer Hotel who are willing to go the extra mile for some dough."

"What are you talking about?" Elias's heart raced anxiously as he replayed Saturday night in his head. The hotel was plagued with cameras, and he was discreet until he reached Ava's room. What type of evidence did Mike have? A kiss could be easily explained, but something more would tear at the seam.

"Nothing happened," he hissed, "and if I read anything about this in your article, I will sue you for defamation."

Mike's grin got wider. "Calm down, mate. Only yanking your chain." He spun on his heels. "I'll call you soon. Got an article to write!"

Chapter 12

Ava stretched out across the mattress like a cat, grinning wickedly at the hot body standing in front of her. Butt naked, Liam searched the room for his discarded clothes. His back was a patchwork of scratches and bites from their passionate lovemaking. The sheets smelled of perfume and sweat with an undertone of sex. She had to get out of the habit of calling Liam when she needed a warm body. Her black book of lovers was almost bursting but he was reliant and accessible, abandoning everything else for a roll in the hay. However, there was one man she wanted to call before considering her ex. She just didn't think Elias would accept her offer.

Ava rolled onto her stomach and reached for her mobile on the bedside table. It was six a.m. "Liam, I gotta get ready for work. I'm running late."

Liam picked up his T-shirt hanging off the dresser. "Is that your subtle way of kicking me out?"

Ava climbed off the bed and gave him a curt kiss on his cheek. "Yes, it is. But don't get used to sleeping over. Last night was a one-time thing."

"You say that every time we hook up."

"I mean it this time." Ava walked into the bathroom and closed the door.

"Have you met someone?" Liam inquired on the other side. "You always give me the cold shoulder when you've slept with another guy."

Ava stared at herself in the mirror, observing her wild, tangled hair and kiss-stained mouth. All she could think about was Elias. Ever since their night together his face had plagued her memory. She wanted him. Wanted more.

"It's none of your business." She waited a beat as she turned on the shower. "I'm taking my car into work so you'll have to find your way to the office."

When Ava exited the bathroom ten minutes later, Liam was gone. She dressed, put on her makeup, and picked up a takeaway coffee at the café down the road.

Elias was already sitting at his desk when she walked into the office. He was dressed in a dark-blue business suit that matched the hue of his eyes. His black hair was brushed off his forehead. He glanced up when she entered and smiled.

"Good morning, Ava."

"Morning, Elias. You had a good weekend at your parents'?"

"It was interesting."

"Why do you say that?"

He tossed her a rolled-up newspaper. "I got propositioned yesterday by an eager journalist."

"Oh?" Ava sat down at her desk and opened the newspaper. "What am I looking for?"

"Go to page six."

She hastily flipped through *The Coastal Times* and gasped at Elias's face splashed across the two-page spread. "What is this? I didn't authorise any press."

"I didn't have a choice," Elias argued. "I was having breakfast with Mum when a journalist named Mike Cordon appeared at the table asking for an impromptu interview."

Ava rolled her eyes. "Jesus, not him again. I thought it might've been Mike when I saw the paper."

"Do you have history?"

"Mike was fresh out of university when he called one day looking for a story. Apparently, I didn't get the memo because Mike's persistence had rippled across the publishing world, pissing a lot of editors off. He was desperate to bring anything to his new boss. So I obliged and he attached to me like a weed. Mike's like a bad smell. You can't get rid of him."

"He was very insistent," Elias remarked. "In fact, he took a seat and joined Mum and I like we'd invited him."

Ava shook her head distastefully. "I'm familiar with the leeches who write for *Coastal Times*. In the past, I've been approached at the salon or petrol station. Nothing stops them when it comes to a story."

"Are you angry at me for doing it?" Elias asked.

"It depends on what he wrote in the article." Ava sipped her coffee and read the headline under her breath: **Young Gun Saves Disgraced Publisher.** The article was well written, showcasing Elias in an attractive and professional light. "*Don't let his cool, blue eyes fool you,*" she continued out loud. "*Elias Dorne may not be making waves in the publishing world yet, but the twenty-seven-year-old is riding the wave to success. As the second-in-command under Blue Tail Media CEO Ava Wolfe, Dorne built a career from the cinders of the nationalised Bobby Hayes scandal. With his extensive background in the industry, he rescued the sinking ship Wolfe spent months trying to salvage.*" Ava lowered the paper and locked a hardened gaze on Elias. "What is this bullshit? You didn't save this company. I did!"

"Calm down, I didn't know he was going to write that," he shot back, looking genuinely hurt at her response. "In fact, I spoke very little at all." He approached her desk and tapped the article. "I was very careful in what I said, Ava. I know the company is recovering but I thought it was a good opportunity to promote Blue Tail positively. It's another form of advertising."

"I can see hardly any mention of Blue Tail," Ava argued. "This article is practically a dating profile! Look, he's listed your likes, dislikes, what you do on the weekends." She paused as she skimmed the page, her lips twitching upwards. "But I cannot see any mention of Daisy."

"I didn't disclose our relationship."

"Why not?"

"He didn't ask and it's none of Cordon's business." A muscle ticked in Elias's jaw as he sat back down at his desk. "If you read the article, you will find that your name is mentioned more times than mine."

A flame of hope ignited in Ava's chest at the nonchalance in his voice. "I would expect so. I practically built your image."

He smiled at her cheeky wink. "Anyway, the article should help with exposure so I'm going to let this one slide. Next time, I expect a call." Ava finished her coffee and made a few phone calls to advertisers, keeping Elias's strong silhouette in her peripheral vision. His mere presence had made her stomach flutter when she skimmed the article when he wasn't looking. He had called her a strategic businesswoman, which was one of the nicest things anyone had said about her. Every word written or said about her had a critical undertone. She couldn't do anything right in the eyes of the public or the board. But she always had Elias's loyalty. Their relationship had blossomed way before their liaison at the fundraiser. She felt safe and human around him. She wanted him so much it hurt. There was only one obstacle in the way: Daisy.

Her office phone buzzed and she welcomed the distraction, picking up the receiver. "Good morning, this is Ava."

"Miss Wolfe, my name is Mary. I'm calling from Event Sydney. How are you?"

Ava bit back a sigh, wondering how an unsolicited phone call made it past the girl outside her office. "I'm well, but I cannot talk right now. I'll transfer you back to my receptionist."

"Miss Wolfe," Mary insisted, "I promise to be quick. We're running a social media seminar in Long River Valley next weekend and I wanted to offer you a place. You have attended our seminars in the past and may be interested in our experienced speakers."

Ava's gaze flicked towards Elias as he worked opposite her. Attending the seminar may be a perfect opportunity to spend quality time with him without their lovers. "How many tickets are available?"

"I've reserved two tickets for you," Mary explained. "However, I cannot hold them for long so I need an answer by close of business today."

"Give my receptionist all the details," Ava replied without a second thought. "I'll make payment this afternoon."

"Can I have the name of your plus-one so I can update your itinerary?"

"Certainly. His name is Elias Dorne."

~ ~ ~

Heavy drops of rain splattered the windscreen as Elias drove the long, ribboned road towards Long River Valley. Beside him, Daisy hummed along to her MP3 player with one headphone bud in her ear. A tourist brochure was spread opened in her lap.

"Elias, did you know that Rosewood Hotel has an Olympic-sized swimming pool and a tennis court. I haven't played since I was ten years old!"

"We can play a game after the seminar," he said, navigating around a bend. "It's only a one-day event so we'll have the rest of the weekend to ourselves."

Her fingers brushed his groin as she squeezed his upper thigh. "Thank you for asking me along this weekend. The girls in the office were jealous when I told them where I was going. I'm so excited!"

Elias scanned the dense bushland, grateful to be away from the concrete jungle. While it was still a working weekend, he looked forward to waking up to native bird calls, kangaroos feasting in the orchards, and early morning runs. "Look, I know things have been hostile between us lately so I thought time away would do some good. We've never been to wine country before. It will be an experience for both of us."

Daisy unplugged her headphones and wound them around her MP3 player. "I'm not picking a fight but"—she dropped her device into her handbag—"is Ava bringing a guest?"

Elias wanted to curse at the sound of Ava's name on Daisy's lips, but he buried the notion. He had invited Daisy to settle the dust, to mend new wounds. He knew that it would take more than a weekend away to reclaim Daisy's trust, but he hoped both of them could move on.

"She's invited her ex-husband," he replied, with a bitter undertone. "Liam has played a big role in the company's expansion and Ava thought he would benefit from the seminar."

"Are they getting back together?"

"I don't know. She hasn't said anything to me."

They crested a hill and Long River Valley emerged from the sleet of rain. Nestled in a sweeping mountain range, the popular tourist destination was known for its lush wineries, hot balloon rides, animal sanctuaries, and the rippling Long River that cut the wine region down the middle. Elias drove into the valley, keeping an eye out for Ava's black Mercedes. In the back of his mind, he'd hoped she and Liam had taken separate cars.

"Are we there yet?" Daisy's voice distracted him from his thoughts.

Elias scanned the passing signs and laughed. "Just

around the corner, Daisy. The hotel is in the middle of town so it won't be hard to miss."

Then, Elias's mobile phone vibrated in the centre console and Daisy instantly reached for it. When her lips hardened into a scowl, he guessed who the caller was.

"Who is it?"

"Your boss. Do you want me to answer it?"

"Yeah, Ava's probably gotten lost." Elias eavesdropped on Daisy's conversation as he turned into the hotel's parking lot, listening for any judgment or prejudice in his girlfriend's voice. To his surprise, it sounded like the two women were getting along.

Daisy threw her head back and laughed. "I know, right! The traffic was a bitch, wasn't it? We've just arrived. Okay, we'll see you when you get here."

"What did she want?" Elias questioned as Daisy ended the call.

"Ava asked if you could order champagne for her room when you check in? She said we can have a drink together when she arrives."

"Did she say if Liam was with her?"

"No, but I heard a man's voice in the background. It was probably him."

Elias parked the car and carried their luggage into the lobby. After checking in and ordering Ava's champagne, he followed Daisy upstairs to their room. The plush carpet cushioned his feet as he strolled the stark-white hallway. Paintings of fruit bowls hung neatly on the walls.

They reached Room 103 and unpacked their belongings to the sweet sounds of birdsong in the trees opposite their balcony.

Daisy flopped onto the king-sized bed and shut her eyes, smiling ear to ear. "This place is amazing! It's going to be such a fabulous weekend." She rolled onto her stomach and hitched her head in her hands, watching Elias unpack. "When does the seminar start?"

"Ten a.m."

A cheeky grin spread across Daisy's face as she unbuttoned her cardigan seductively, her green gaze unwavering. Tossing the garment across the room, she purred, "Do we have time for some fun in the Jacuzzi before you leave?"

Elias didn't need to ponder the invitation. He unshed his clothes and jumped into bed, lowering his warm body onto hers, rewarding Daisy with a passionate kiss. "There's always time."

Chapter 13

"How's Daisy enjoying the hotel?" Ava asked Elias as they followed the crowd into the conference room. A sizable stage took up space at the far end of the room, adorned with a black and white banner with the words: **OPTIMISE YOUR SOCIAL MEDIA PRESENCE.**

The room was bustling with business people in casual clothes, cradling tablets, notepads, and booklets handed to them by ushers at the door.

"She's spending the entire day by the pool," Elias replied. "With her fair skin, she's going to cook under the sun."

"It was very sweet of you to invite her." Ava manoeuvred through a group of people congregating in the aisle. "I gather the girl doesn't get out much."

Elias followed her to their seats five rows from the stage. "She's very excitable, that's all."

"I look forward to meeting her at dinner."

"Are you serious? Or is it some ploy to suss out the competition?"

Ava turned to him, her luscious mouth opened in shock. "I am offended, Elias. You've told me so much about her that I wanted to meet Daisy in person. Is that a crime? I have no ulterior motive, I swear."

"There you are." Liam squeezed down the aisle and took the empty seat next to Ava. He leaned over her to shake Elias's hand. "Good to see you again, mate. Did you find the hotel okay?"

"I had my trusty GPS."

"We got lost, didn't we, babe?" Liam patted Ava's thigh, locking gazes with Elias. "My GPS is so old it didn't recognise the new roads that were built four years ago."

Biting at his lip to divert the jealousy, Elias drew his gaze to the floor-length windows. Thick, heavy clouds formed on the horizon. A thunderstorm was on its way. He wanted to have a swim before it started raining, but the seminar was already running ten minutes late. Elias pulled out his phone and texted Daisy. She didn't respond straight away, replying when the lights dimmed.

Daisy: When do you break for lunch?
Elias: One o'clock. There's a storm coming. Be safe
Daisy: I will. Have fun

He pocketed his phone and unpacked his notepad and pens, eager for the seminar to start so he could take advantage of the mini holiday. Music played from the speakers surrounding the room and the host stepped onto the stage, waving at the crowd. For the next two hours, Elias tried his hardest to concentrate, keeping one eye on the impending storm and the other on Liam's wandering hands. His entire body grew rigid at the sight of Liam's fingers caressing the soft skin on Ava's thigh. He couldn't justify how he felt for her, ashamed for his body's reaction whenever she was near. Today, she wasn't helping his resolve at all. Ava looked breathtaking in casual attire, dressed in a floral skirt that showed off her slim legs. Her hair was unrestrained, falling around her face in copper curls.

Her gaze slewed to the side, catching him staring, and she rewarded him with a ghost of a smile. "Why are you looking at me like that?" she whispered.

"I didn't know I was staring."

"Subtlety was never in your repertoire, Elias," Ava said with a giggle. "Are you enjoying the seminar? I think it's very informative."

Elias glanced down at his blank notepad and frowned. "It's a little repetitive. I studied social media at university but a lot has changed in the industry since then."

A clap of thunder exploded above the ceiling, momentarily startling everyone in the room.

"We'll stop here for lunch, folks," the host declared. "There are sandwiches, tea, and coffee in the mess hall down the corridor. Please return to your seat by two o'clock."

Elias couldn't get out of the room quick enough, ignoring Ava's calls above the hubbub. He marched to the entrance of the building and pushed the doors open. Heavy rain pelted the car park, creating small dams in the golf course opposite the conference hall.

Elias exhaled until his lungs were empty, disappointed his plans for a swim were thwarted. He pulled out his phone and called Daisy. It rang out. She was probably running back to the hotel room.

He was readying himself for a dash across the car park when Ava materialised next to him. "Are you making a break for it?" she asked.

"I'm heading back to Daisy. I cannot stand to sit for another minute in that seminar. I was getting claustrophobic."

"We can leave if you want," she offered. "To be honest, I only bought the tickets as an excuse to get away from the city. They won't know we're gone."

"What about Liam?"

Ava's eyebrows snapped together. "What about him? He can stay if he wants. He needs to be more fluent in social media anyway."

They stood in silence for a few moments, watching the rain sweep across the plump wineries. A bolt of lightning erupted in the sky, making them both jump.

"Are you ready?" Ava took Elias's hand and held it tightly. "I don't think the rain will ease up any time soon. We must go now!"

"What direction is the hotel?" Elias asked, squinting into the deluge. It was so thick, he couldn't see two feet in front of him.

Ava laughed and pulled at his arm. "Elias, we don't have time to navigate. Let's go!" She dragged him into the onslaught, squealing like a child when the cold rain drenched her. Elias followed her closely, keeping their fingers entwined, enjoying how her shirt moulded to her wet body. Thunder rolled above their heads, violent and angry. Lightning split the sky, sparking in the air seemingly metres away.

"Ava, it's not safe out here," Elias shouted. "We have to go back to the conference hall."

She slowed to a jog and frantically searched her surroundings. They had run in the opposite direction of the hotel, ending up at the far end of the car park near a maintenance shed.

"In here!" Elias hauled Ava to the front door of the building and jiggled the handle. It swung open. He pushed her inside and latched the door closed. The small windows let enough fractured light in to search for blankets stored on the shelves.

"Here, this should warm you up until the storm clears." He wrapped a blanket around Ava's trembling shoulders, ushering her to an old garden bench pressed against the wall.

"Are you all right?" he asked.

"A little wet but I'll survive."

"What have we learned from this experience?"

"Never to go swimming in a downpour again?"

"That's right." He joined her on the bench, shoulder to shoulder, swaddling himself in the dank, smelly blanket. The rain tapped melodically on the tin roof, drowning out the chorus of frogs and crickets.

"I didn't bring Liam here to spite you," Ava said quietly, kicking off her drenched high heels.

"Why did you?"

She diverted her gaze to the ground, kneading her fingers into a ball. "As a distraction, I guess. I couldn't bear looking at you and Daisy together."

"You were the one who suggested we bring our partners."

"I'm not dating Liam," Ava announced, "just sleeping with him."

Elias let out a frustrated growl and stood up, pushing the blanket off his shoulders. He paced the garden shed, keeping his eyes off Ava's diminutive form. "Why did you tell me that? I don't want to know about you and him." He brushed his wet hair off his forehead in one sweep. "Look, Ava. I can't explain what's going on between us. Ever since we since slept together, I can't get you out of my head. You're like a poison that has taken over my body. I can't function when you're around."

She stood up to join him, snaking her arms around his waist, pressing her chest against his. "You're bad for me, Elias. I've never felt this way about anyone before, not even my ex-husband." She leaned in until their lips almost brushed. "I want your body, Elias."

"You had me once and I swore that would be the last time. I'm with Daisy now, Ava. I can't betray her again."

"Do you love her?"

"We're going to get married one day."

"That's not the same thing. Do you love her?"

All Elias could hear was Ava's rapid breathing when he grazed her bottom lip with the pad of his thumb. Then, he tasted his finger, the saltiness of her skin igniting the fire in his belly. "You drive me fucking crazy."

He smashed his lips against hers, burying his tongue into the sweet depths of her mouth. Ava moaned deep in her throat, her body weakening at his touch. Elias grew mad with hunger, stripping the blanket off Ava's shoulders, yearning to touch her body underneath. Looping one arm around her waist, he feathered kisses along her jawline, kneading her breast through the thin material of her shirt.

The pounding of the rain intensified when he stripped the garment off Ava's body, revealing her full breasts in a red lace bra. She shivered at her near nakedness, watching Elias remove his shirt and tossing it aside. He explored the planes of her back, the curves of her buttocks with greedy hands, reaching underneath her skirt to slip off her underwear. He stilled when a noise of protest left her lips.

"Do you want me to stop?" he whispered. "We don't have to do this."

"No, keep going."

He unfolded the blankets onto the floor and lowered her gently onto the makeshift mattress. With trembling fingers, Ava unhooked his belt buckle and unzipped his fly, wrapping her cold hand around his member. Elias gasped at her touch and pulled down his pants to his knees. He hovered over her, admiring the shivering, beautiful creature underneath him. Her emerald eyes were round and wild, two beacons leading him into the storm.

He entered her body slowly, filling her until her screams were muted by the thunder. She felt silky and warm. Ava closed her eyes and wrapped her legs around his hips, forcing him to go deeper. Elias swept her hair back from her cheeks, affectionately kissing her temple. There were a hundred things he wanted to say to her at that moment. The word *love* lingered on his tongue. He wasn't sure where this was taking him or what would happen when they returned to their partners. But Elias knew in his heart that he couldn't bear to be without her.

Stabilising both hands on the concrete, Elias thrusted harder and deeper, driving into Ava as she clawed her fingers down his back. Above them, the rain eased, the storm dissipating. Beams of sunlight streamed through the windows.

Rolling waves of pleasure swelled inside Elias, controlling every breath, every heartbeat. He welcomed his release, filling Ava with his warmth. Her body shuddered underneath him as she climaxed soon after, her hips arched against his, her arms still wrapped around his waist.

Elias looked down at her face, seeing fragility and innocence in her eyes. As much as he tried to deny it, he was in love with Ava Wolfe.

~ ~ ~

The hotel room was empty when Ava made it back, half dressed and looking a complete mess. Her shirt was ruined, her makeup was smeared across her face, and she was certain her Jimmy Choo shoes were unrepairable.

She shared a private giggle with herself as she closed the door behind her and wandered into the bathroom. What a wild—and unexpected—afternoon. Making love in a dusty, dirty shed was at the bottom of her to-do list, but being with Elias released a kinky and uninhibited side to her.

She turned on the shower and made sure the water was scalding hot before dipping underneath the stream. Her back ached from lying on the hard ground and her most intimate part still tingled. She felt like a teenager coming home from a forbidden night out with the neighbourhood bad boy. Liam hadn't bothered to call while she was out, probably sitting at the bar drinking away his troubles. She still couldn't understand why she kept him hanging around. Maybe it was for validation. Either way, it was time to let him go.

Ava washed her hair, rinsed, and turned off the shower. She stepped into the walk-in wardrobe, naked, searching for a dress to wear for dinner tonight. She wanted to look good for Elias and even better for Daisy. There was nothing wrong with healthy competition.

The front door opened and footsteps ascended the hall towards her. "Ava, are you back yet?"

"I'm in the bedroom, Liam," Ava called back, picking out her favourite Gucci dress. It cost a fortune, but it moulded to her body like a dream and gave the public a generous view of her breasts. She was zipping it up when Liam entered the room.

"Where have you been?" he demanded, his dark eyes frantic. "I had half the hotel staff looking for you. You disappeared into the storm and I thought the worst."

"I was with Elias. We found shelter in a maintenance shed." She turned her back on him as she slipped into her high heels. The heat of his stare burned into her neck. "We waited there until the storm passed. I'm sorry I didn't call you."

"What were you doing with Elias?" Accusation dripped from his lips.

Ava sidestepped him to get to the bathroom. "I don't have to explain myself to you," she said, digging around in her makeup case. "You're not my husband anymore. Elias was heading back to Daisy and I needed to get something from our room. We just happened to leave at the same time."

Liam lent a shoulder on the door frame, arms crossed over his chest. "You were gone for an hour. No one knew where you were."

"Did people look for Elias as well?"

"We just assumed you were together."

"We?"

"Daisy and me," Liam said. "We got talking in the foyer earlier. You know, she's a charming girl. Elias is lucky to have her."

Ava applied her lipstick, watching Liam's reflection in the mirror. He was dressed in a suit and tie, looking dapper as usual. His cheeks were flushed red so her theory about him drinking at the bar was right. "Did I miss anything important at the seminar?"

"Nah, it was stuff you already knew. Social media hasn't really changed in the last two years. But I took notes so I'll email them to you later."

"Thanks."

Silence hung heavy in the air as she finished her makeup. Now would be the perfect time to dump Liam. They were heading home tomorrow and she could take back her spare house key when he wasn't looking. She could start Monday with a clean slate.

"Liam, I wanted to speak to you about—"

He pushed off the door frame, stepping into the bathroom. "Actually, I wanted to speak to you first."

"About?"

He reached over and plucked her mascara from her fingers. Doubt settled like a rock in her chest and she hoped he wasn't dumping her. They still had dinner to sit through.

"It's about Elias," Liam said.

Ava heaved a sigh and snapped back her mascara, the heaviness in her chest lifting. "Of course it is. What's wrong now?"

Liam cleared his throat. "Look, I don't know what you two have going on, but he won't hang around for long."

"What the fuck do you mean?"

"You break things, Ava. You treat men like toys. You pick them up, play with them, and put them back down again broken and scarred. That's what you did to me. You break hearts and you will break his."

"Since when do you care about Elias?"

"I cared the moment you fell in love with him. I see it on your face, Ava. The man has captivated you . . . like I once did." Liam spun on his heels and left the bathroom, calling out from the other room. "I'll meet you down in the restaurant. Take your time getting ready for *him*."

Chapter 14

Ava stood in the doorway of the restaurant and searched the dimly lit tables for Elias and Liam. The orchestral tunes of Mozart played softly, creating a romantic ambience for the couples sitting around the room. Waiters zipped around carrying plates of food and drink.

Unable to find the maître d', Ava made her way through the restaurant, ignoring the inquisitive stares from other diners. She was used to people staring. It was part of being the CEO to a nationally discredited company.

But sleeping with Elias felt as though she was brandished with a scarlet letter. Could people see the fear and guilt lying underneath her skin? Her career had been built by making mistakes and fixing them. If word got out she was screwing her staff and ruining relationships, her life as a CEO would be over.

"Ava, over here, honey!" Liam's loud voice cut through the ambience. She smiled when she saw Elias sitting at the table, dressed in a dark suit, his ink-black hair combed off his forehead. His lips twitched upwards before vanishing when Daisy leaned into view.

Stiffened by nerves, Ava studied the stunning blonde at the table. All she saw were boobs and attitude. Her burgundy gown rivalled an A-lister's dress at an award show and her neck dripped in sparkling diamonds. All though she was overdressed for the Italian restaurant, Daisy looked breathtaking.

Ava sat between Liam and Elias, noticing a glass of white

wine perspiring in front of her. She must've been staring at it for some time because Daisy made the first move.

"It's chardonnay imported from France," she explained. "Elias and I bought it ages ago and never had an occasion to drink it." She grinned widely at Elias and squeezed his hand. "It's a special weekend so I thought it would be good to bring it along."

"That was very kind of you," Ava said, picking up her glass. The heat of Elias's stare burned into her as she drained the entire glass in one gulp. She would need something stronger if she was going to survive the dinner. She attracted the attention of a waiter and gave him an order. "I would like a glass of whiskey and a bottle of Moet for the table, please." She turned to the others. "Would you like anything?"

Elias, Liam, and Daisy shook their heads and the waiter departed for the bar.

"I believe the most beautiful women in this room are sitting at our table," Liam said proudly. "Don't you agree, Elias?"

Elias's lips flickered downwards before taking a sip of wine. "We certainly do."

"There's a group of men sitting in the corner staring at us," Liam observed, jabbing a thumb over his shoulder. "I may have to fight them off with a stick!"

Daisy's girlish laughter echoed around the table. "You're such a charmer, Liam."

Ava resisted the urge to roll her eyes, exhaling with relief when her whiskey arrived. She took the glass out of the waiter's hand and dunk it back. The alcohol burned down her throat, the perfect distraction to Liam and Daisy battering eyelashes at each other.

Elias leaned over and whispered in her ear, "The bottom of my shower is covered in dirt and sawdust."

Ava stifled a laugh. "How's that possible? I was the one on the floor."

He grinned wickedly at her. "It was the best afternoon of my life."

"Did you tell Daisy what happened?"

"About us sleeping together?"

"No! I meant the garden shed."

"She knows we got stuck in the rain and found shelter. That's it."

"Did she tell you that half of the hotel staff were looking for us? Liam told me there was a search party."

A blush crept into his cheeks. "No, she didn't. I was indisposed at the time." Ava popped open the Moet and poured herself a drink, ignoring the three other glasses on the table. "Let's order, shall we?"

While the waiter took their orders, Ava felt Elias's warm breath on her ear. "What is wrong with you?" he hissed. "Are you angry at me because I slept with my girlfriend?"

"I'm angry because you just slept with me!" Luckily, her outburst was muted by a trio of waiters singing happy birthday to the table beside them.

Ava pushed her chair back and charged to the ladies' bathroom. She planted her hands on the basin and stared at her reflection in the mirror, hating the woman staring back. How could she fall in love with a man like Elias? He was her employee. Nothing more. She had broken boundaries in the past and vowed to never let a man sway her to the bedroom. But Elias had a gravitational pull on her unlike anyone else. Their feelings for each other grew every day and there were times Ava had to restrain herself from making another mistake.

However, she couldn't deny the hurt in her chest when he'd had sex with Daisy after sleeping with her. How could she define their relationship? It was purely business, wasn't it?

The bathroom door swung open and Daisy entered, a concerned look plastered across her painted face. "Are you all right? You left the table so quickly."

Ava splashed cold water on her face. "Just man troubles."

"What did Liam do?"

Ava exhaled a long breath and turned her back on her reflection. "Do you often feel that love is one-sided? You spend so much effort making that one person a part of your world, only for them to deny your feelings?"

"Is this about Liam?" Daisy asked, pulling a paper towel from the dispenser for her. "He wants to get back together."

"He told you that?"

"He was pretty freaked out when we couldn't find you during the storm. He told me all about how you met, your wedding, and how much he misses you since the divorce. He still loves you, Miss Wolfe."

Ava took the paper towel from Daisy and dabbed her eyes. "Call me Ava."

"Do you still love him?"

The echo of her words to Elias forced a new wave of tears to her eyes. "I don't know how I feel. I've been so consumed by rebuilding this company that my personal life was put on hold."

Daisy smiled and rested a hand on Ava's shoulder. "I would like us to be friends, Ava. Let's swap numbers. You can call me anytime you want to bitch about men. Trust me, I have my fair share of frustrations."

"What has Elias ever done to you? He's—" Ava caught herself before saying the word *perfect*. He was perfect in her eyes because he kept his mouth shut and compiled to her advances. There was so much more she wanted to explore with him. "He cares deeply for you. I know that much."

Daisy's lips pursed together as a darkness clouded her eyes. "Elias is not perfect, Ava. He takes forever to commit. Believe me, I've been waiting for him to ask me out for three years. It's not other women that distract him. It's his work. The day he got the job at Blue Tail was the moment I started to lose him. You saw Elias more than I did."

"I'm partially to blame for that."

"You know, there was a part of me that believed you and Elias were having an affair," Daisy said. "You guys spent so much time together that I was convinced he was cheating. But that's ridiculous because Elias prefers blondes."

Ava was certain Daisy's little jab was meant to be innocent but she took offence to it. She tossed her paper towel into the trash and headed for the door. "Elias isn't cheating on you with me," she said. "But you better keep an eye on him. I heard a rumour he was getting friendly with a blonde from Accounts." She took pleasure in the look of shock on Daisy's face as they returned to the table. Their food was waiting for them.

"Best friends now?" Liam quizzed, tucking his napkin into his shirt. The aroma of his lamb shanks encircled the table.

Still white faced, Daisy simply nodded and drained her glass of wine.

"What did you say to her?" Elias whispered to Ava.

Ava picked up her fork and swirled it around her fettuccine. "Nothing incriminating. She doesn't believe that you and I had an affair."

"Oh, it was that easy?"

"I just diverted the blame."

"What?"

"I would like to propose a toast!" Liam thrust his glass in the air and waited until the others did the same. "To the future. Where our lovers are the truest, our friends the staunchest, and our bank accounts the largest!"

By the time dessert rolled around, Ava couldn't bear to look at the tiramisu or sticky date pudding on the menu. The mix of Moet and rich fettuccine formed a greasy ball in her gut. She had considered ordering a whiskey and going to bed early if it wasn't for the sight of Daisy and Elias slow dancing across from her.

"If you keep staring at him like that, you're going to bore holes in the floor." Liam's voice sounded in her ear.

"Go away, Liam," she hissed, recoiling at his alcoholic breath. "You're drunk."

"I'm only trying to help you, Ava," he responded, his voice slurred. "I see the way you look at him." He leaned in closer. "Tell me. Do you think of Elias when we fuck?"

Ava exhaled a breath of hot air and pushed him away. "Go to bed," she ordered. "You're embarrassing yourself."

"I'll go upstairs when you admit it."

"Admit what?"

"It's obvious, isn't it? You're in love with Elias!"

A squeal of delight erupted over the orchestral music. A frenzied Daisy pushed her way through the dancers towards the table. "Oh my God, Ava," she screamed. "Ava, look!" She shoved her hand into the woman's face. Ava stared at the rock glittering on Daisy's left hand and felt her world shatter around her into a million pieces.

~ ~ ~

"Mum, what about this one?" Daisy cried, pointing to an open bridal magazine. "I've always loved the halter-neck style."

"Choose what will make you comfortable, honey," her mother said. "You'll be wearing it all day."

Hiding behind a tower of bridal and wedding magazines, Elias bit at his lip, mindlessly flipping through venue brochures. All he could think about was the expression on Ava's face when she saw the diamond ring on Daisy's finger. He didn't know what he was thinking proposing to her. It was a foolish move on his part, swept up in the moment.

As much as he loved Daisy, thoughts of Ava had haunted his memory. Both women offered something to him the other couldn't provide. Daisy provided balance and stability, while Ava gave him a few nights of hot, passionate sex.

He had feelings for both women, but he chose to give the ring to Daisy because he didn't see his fling with Ava going anywhere once he put his resignation in.

He had decided to quit the moment he stepped out of the garden shed with Ava. Their relationship was becoming toxic and dependable. They would only destroy each other. It would be for the best. He just needed to tell his fiancée.

"Elias, have you seen anything you like?" Daisy asked.

"I'm not supposed to see the dress, aren't I?" he groaned. "I don't understand why I'm even here."

"We need your help with choosing a venue," Olivia remarked, dropping another mound of brochures in front of him. "It's your day too. Do you prefer a beachside wedding or a church wedding?"

Elias stared at the burgeoning pile of brochures and picked one out at random. "What about this place?"

Daisy and her mother inspected it closely, mumbling to each other. "I do like the idea of combining the ceremony and reception into one venue," Daisy said. "It's classy and a little less traditional than a church. What do you think, babe?"

"I'm leaving the venue in your hands." Elias leaned over the table and stroked her cheek. "As long as I get to spend the day with you, I don't mind where we get married." His mobile buzzed in his pocket and he took the welcome distraction to duck out of the room to answer it. "Hello, Ava. Is everything all right?"

Her line was silent for a few moments before she answered. "I'm sorry to bother you on Sunday but I didn't congratulate you on your engagement." Ava's voice sounded emotionless and cold. "The week after the seminar was so busy that it slipped my mind."

"I know, Ava. I was there with you."

"Have you set a date?"

"Not yet. Daisy and I have spent the entire weekend looking at wedding magazines and we haven't decided on the month. If I see one more venue brochure, I think I'm going to lose my mind."

"Let Daisy have her fun. Planning a wedding is a wonderful yet stressful time. She needs you to be cooperative. But when you see her walking down the aisle in her white dress, it will all be worth it."

"You never talk about your wedding to Liam," Elias observed.

"Why would I? It's my private business. Anyway, it ended in divorce. Marriage isn't for everyone."

Elias walked to the sliding door that led into the backyard and stepped outside. The sun beat down from above, warming the pavement under his feet as he paced the yard. "Look, Ava. We need to talk about what happened at the dinner. You were in meetings all week so I didn't have a chance to talk to you."

"Elias, there's nothing to discuss. It just came as a shock because you never mentioned you were planning to propose. I thought you and I—"

He let out a long breath. "I want to discuss it because it obviously affects you. I can't explain what you and I have but it shouldn't have never happened. You're my employer. We work too closely together for any relationship to work." He kicked a boot into the grass, spreading wet earth across the lawn. "What would people think if our relationship was ever leaked? It would destroy the company."

"I don't fucking care what people think, Elias," Ava cried. "We're both to blame for what happened. We're both adulterers. Do you regret sleeping with me?"

Elias chose his next words carefully. There were times where he'd regretted succumbing to her—twice—but they had come together when they needed someone the most.

"Ava, meeting you and working for Blue Tail have been the best days of my life. I can't take that away."

"Why did you do it?" Ava asked. "Why did you propose to Daisy? You don't even love her."

"I shouldn't have to explain myself to you," he barked. "You and I were never exclusive. It was just an affair. For your information, I do love Daisy. She can give me a future, Ava. I don't see a future with you."

"I know how you feel about me." Ava's voice trembled as she tried to restrain her emotions. "By marrying Daisy, you're only making things worse. You only proposed to her to hide your true feelings for me. That poor girl deserves a chance."

"I am giving her a chance!"

The sliding door opened, and Daisy popped her head out. "Is everything all right, Elias? We heard shouting."

He planted on a fake smile. "I'm okay. It's just a business call. I'll be right in."

"Don't be too long. Mum's chocolate chip cookies are almost ready."

"Okay, honey." He waited until Daisy retreated back inside before returning to Ava. "Look, I've been doing a lot of thinking. Things between you and I have progressed a lot further than we ever anticipated. It's not going to work if we're stuck in the same office every day."

Her end went silent. "Is this your resignation?"

"I think it's best."

"If that's what you want. I can't stop you. Don't worry about the two weeks' notice. I'll send a courier to deliver your belongings to your apartment this week."

"I'll work the week, Ava. I need to finalise things with my clients, anyway."

"No, it's not necessary. As you said, it won't be healthy for us to be stuck in a room together."

"Ava, please."

"Good luck for your future wedding, Elias. It's been wonderful working with you."

When he heard the dial tone in his ear, Elias felt as though he had destroyed the one thing that made him feel alive.

Chapter 15

"Miss Wolfe, your eleven o'clock interview is here," the receptionist said, popping her head into the office.

With her eyes focused on a magazine layout, Ava responded sharply, "Remind me, Sally. Who is it again?"

"Fran Valerie. She applied for Mr. Dorne's position." The receptionist entered the office and placed a résumé beside Ava. "She has ten years' experience working beside Lance Henn at Hope Publications and has an extensive copywriting background."

"How old is she?"

"Did you have a chance to read her résumé? Normally, Elias would've looked after this . . ." She trailed off when Ava locked a hardened gaze on her.

"No, Sally, I haven't had time to read résumés," Ava snapped. "It's your job to manage the hiring process. I thought you were capable to doing it. But if you cannot complete a simple task, I will choose someone else."

Elias's absence in the office had not only left a gaping hole in workload but also in Ava's frame of mind. Over the last three weeks, she found herself surrendering to the job completely, dedicating long hours at the office, submitting magazines to print, writing emails, or taking conference calls, often staying until midnight.

The nagging headaches and sickness in her stomach were signs to slow down. But she couldn't. In truth, she feared coming home to an empty house, because worst of all, she was alone. Work was all she had left.

The receptionist cleared her throat and retreated to the door. "I'll bring Fran in right away, ma'am."

A middle-aged woman carrying a briefcase entered the office and stretched an arm across Ava's desk. "Hi, I'm Fran. Thank you for seeing me this morning."

"Please take a seat."

Fran obeyed, sitting opposite her. There was a day where Elias had sat in that very spot, his wide, cobalt-blue eyes piercing her cold exterior. Ava tried hard to push those memories deeper into her subconscious. She picked up Fran's résumé and skimmed over it. "Has Sally explained the role to you?" she asked.

"Yes, I practically memorised the job description," Fran replied proudly, pushing her glasses up the bridge of her nose. "I understand it's a communications management position involving copywriting and sales and marketing."

"That's correct. This is a newly created position, broken down from a much larger one. The role involves working long hours and you must be on call twenty-four/seven. You'll be provided with a new mobile phone upon employment."

Fran's eyebrows quivered for a fraction of a second. "Oh, that wasn't mentioned in the advertisement."

"Will working long hours be a problem for you?" Ava questioned. "The cogs of this company don't stop turning after five p.m., Miss Valerie. There are events to plan and meetings to organise with salesmen in other states. I need someone who is committed and dedicated to working hard." She glanced over the woman's résumé again. "Do you have school-aged children?"

"No, I have two adult boys."

"The reason I ask is because the hours required for this position may not suit candidates with young families."

Fran shifted in her chair and Ava could tell by her constant blinking and thinned lips that the woman had already made her decision. To make the interview—and her time—worth it, she asked Fran a few more questions before ending the interview. "Thank you for coming in, Miss Valerie. I'll be in touch."

The women shook hands and Fran exited the office, softly closing the door behind her. Waiting a beat, Ava reached into the drawer for her silver flask, unscrewing it hastily. The warming taste of bourbon scalded her throat as it slipped down. There was always alcohol stored in her office for entertaining guests, but Ava found herself reaching for the bottle ever since Elias left. After interviewing other candidates, Ava realised that Elias could never be replaced, and it scared her to think how reliant she'd become on him. His face haunted her thoughts day and night. She could end her suffering by a simple phone call, yet the memory of the diamond ring on Daisy's finger made her reconsider. She wasn't ready to confront her feelings.

Ava swallowed the entire flask and stood up, swaying side to side. She made it to her door, planting two palms against the timber to stabilize herself. She was tipsy, teetering on the edge of drunk. She needed something in her belly before her next meeting. When Ava opened the door, the entire office stilled. She felt the heat of one hundred eyes track her down the hallway towards the kitchen. When Ava turned the corner, she wasn't yet freed from judgement, hearing the hushed chatter of women.

"Something must've gone down between them," a voice said. "They spent a lot of time together at seminars and business trips. I don't think it's normal for colleagues to work so closely together like that. A man and a woman cannot spend all that time together without something happening."

"I wonder if that's why he left." Another voice joined the conversation. "She probably made a move on him. Ava *does* have a certain reputation. Even I knew that before I started working here."

"I heard a rumour she slept with Elias after the fundraiser. They were both plastered."

"Where did you hear that?"

Ava stepped into the kitchen and casually opened the fridge for a bottle of water. "Oh, don't stop on account of me, ladies," she said, turning around to face them. The three women froze at the sight of her, glancing at each other anxiously. She recognised them as Ellen, Stacey, and Emma, the gossiping copywriters in the office.

"We were just talking about—" Ellen began.

Ava shot her hand up, silencing her. "I don't want to hear it. This office has a zero policy on workplace bullying and gossip. I want to see all three of you in my office right now."

Ava marched down the hall with a mixture of satisfaction and pride. She didn't need a man to feel complete. She had built her career from the ground up, stepping over women like Ellen, Stacey, and Emma to get where she was today. Men were distractions and warm bodies to sleep next to. What she had with Elias was just a fling and Ava would move on like she did with all of her lovers. The old Ava was back.

~ ~ ~

Elias couldn't work with clouded focus. He stared at the paragraph typed on the screen in front of him and hit the backspace bar until it was gone. His writing was shit, his eyes hurt, and his heart ached. He missed her. There was no denying it. Ava was the first thing he thought about when he woke up and the last thing before he went to sleep. He felt guilty because his beautiful blonde fiancée should be the one in his thoughts, not his ex-boss.

Their wedding was real and happening. The date was set for six months' time, the venue booked, and Daisy had spent the weekend with her parents searching for a dress. By all accounts, Elias should be excited about his upcoming nuptials, but all he could think about was *her*. There was no way in Hell Daisy would've agreed to send an invitation to Ava, so Elias pushed himself to make contact with her. Would she want to talk to him? Had she moved on with someone else? The notion of Ava being with another man forged a beast inside him. She was never his to begin with, but they had fun together, and she made him feel alive for the first time in years.

His relationship with Daisy was safe so when he left Blue Tail Media, he searched for a job that was also safe. He was headhunted by agencies and publishers until he accepted a position as a senior copywriter at First Words Creative Agency. The money wasn't as good as Blue Tail, but the job was walking distance from his apartment and he managed his own team of writers. He was moving up in the world without the woman he wanted by his side.

He rewrote his paragraph and finished the website copy before lunch. His team of three writers had already departed for the Thai restaurant down the road. Even with an invitation, Elias didn't feel like socialising, spending half the day constructing and deconstructing texts to Ava. What would he say to her? Three weeks had passed without a flicker of communication from both parties. She didn't have any social media, so he couldn't stalk her. The only way to contact Ava was the old-fashioned way—by phone or email.

He opened the drawer for his mobile and called her. His heart beat in time with the dial tone, begging for her to answer. When it rang out, Elias tossed his phone into the drawer and cursed under his breath. He was overreacting. Ava was probably in meetings or at lunch. He knew from experience that she rarely left her phone unattended.

Elias was prepared to ring again when an email pinged at the bottom of his computer screen. It was from Mike Cordon at *The Coastal Times*. Intrigued and a little perturbed that the journo knew his direct email, Elias opened the link in the email body. It took him to the digital version of the newspaper, opened to the societal section.

Featured on a two-page spread was a collection of grainy images of Elias and a faceless woman emerging from the garden shed in Long River Valley. He bit down the urge to vomit as he studied the photographs, wondering how he didn't see the photographer. Luckily, the rain was too heavy and thick for a clear photo of Ava's face.

A surge of anger replaced the feeling of sickness inside him. Elias pounced off his chair to search for Mike's business card in his briefcase. When he found it, his fingers couldn't keep up as he dialled the journalist's number. He picked up after two rings.

"Hello."

"Where the fuck did you get those photographs?"

"Ah, Mr. Dorne. I wondered when I'll hear from you again."

"Where did you get those photographs?" Elias repeated, his hand curling into a fist.

"I can't tell you that, Mr. Dorne. They were sent to me from an anonymous source. They were left on my desk in an envelope yesterday."

"You printed them without permission!"

"I don't respond well to shouting," Mike said coolly. "I'm a journalist, not a priest. I don't need your permission before I print images. Who's the woman, anyway? She's definitely not Daisy. She's blonde."

"No comment."

"Come on, don't play the innocent now. Someone caught you in the middle of forbidden tryst. What exactly were you doing in that shed?"

"You must contact me if you receive any more photographs." Elias's heart was beating so fast that he thought it would burst from of his chest. He couldn't remember any press or paparazzi being at the hotel. The images were taken on a mobile phone, so someone had betrayed him.

"Who's the woman, Mr. Dorne?" Mike questioned. "If you tell me who she is, I won't publish any more photos as they come to me."

"There's more?"

"My source told me so. Look, there's only a small pool of possible suspects and I'm very good at my job. I know you were there for business with Ava Wolfe. Is she the mysterious woman?" His laugh echoed down the line. "But I gotta tell you I was shocked to hear you two went your separate ways after such a public coupling. Why is that?"

"None of your business. Look, I'm at work—"

"Mr. Dorne, you can cooperate, or you can let me do my job. I will find out either way who your mistress is. I deserve a thank you, in fact. I heard you're getting married. Wouldn't it be such a shame if these images got into Daisy's inbox?"

"If they do, I will fucking sue you."

"Calm down. Our readership is too small for the paper to get into Daisy's hands, unless she has friends up here. What's that infamous saying? Keep your friends close, and your enemies closer."

Elias saw his writers come off the lift. He had to end this conversation before too much was overheard. "You told me you had photographic evidence of Ava and me at the fundraiser. Did you really?"

"Are you confirming my suspicions?"

"Tell me, Cordon."

"I never reveal my sources. What I have now is much more damaging than a photo of you and Ava looking cosy."

"What do you want from me?" Elias asked. "Money? Recognition? Or are you just another blood-sucking journalist?"

Silence hung heavy on Mike's end before he finally spoke. "Have a good day, Elias. I will be in touch."

Chapter 16

Ava had better things to do with her time than sit in a three-hour-long board meeting. She still hadn't found a replacement for Elias, which probably explained the unexpected arrival of the board of directors at the office. Chairman Frank Boulder sat at the head of the table, dressed in a freshly pressed black suit and tie. His bald head shone under the yellow ceiling lights. He attended the monthly meetings rarely so she must have fucked up big time for him to be here today.

"Miss Wolfe, I need you to explain your recent staff movements to the board. We agreed with your decision to hire Elias Dorne to assist in rebuilding the company brand. I thought everything was going smoothly until I was informed of his resignation. Can you explain why he quit?"

Ava cleared her throat, avoiding the heated glares from the other board members. If they ever found out the truth, they'll have another scandal on their hands. "He was headhunted," she lied. "I wasn't aware that other agencies were after him. I couldn't persuade him to stay."

"Did you offer him more money?"

"I tried too, but the board rejected my plea. Look, he's not returning my calls so I doubt he'll accept an offer to return."

Silence hung heavy in the air as Frank read from a thick file in front of him. "Have you rehired the position? It's gravely important we get someone in Elias's role immediately. His efforts in rebuilding our damaged name has greatly influenced our stocks and public image. I don't want to waste time and money finding second best." His gaze locked with Ava's. "We've lost an invaluable employee. What are you going to do to rectify this?"

"I've been interviewing potential candidates last week but none had the same standards as Elias. I've been delegating his tasks to other staff at the moment."

"It will have to do for now." Frank sighed heavily. "We'll just have to get a temp in until we can rehire." He turned to his secretary sitting offside and barked orders at her.

Ava reached for her glass of water—wishing it was vodka—and saw her phone light up with a text from Elias. She restrained her excitement while she read his message.

Elias: We need to talk right away
Ava: Not now
Elias: It's not up for discussion, Ava. It's urgent
Ava: I'm in a board meeting. I can't walk out.
Elias: When can I see you?
Ava: Meet me for lunch at Mac's. I'll be there at 2pm
Elias: OK. See you then

"Miss Wolfe, am I interrupting your social life?"

Ava jumped at the sound of his voice and dropped the mobile into her handbag by her feet. "No, Frank. Just news from the office."

"Speaking of that, I heard you fired three copywriters last week. I can understand one, but not three."

"They weren't performing, Frank. I introduced key performance indicators into everyone's job description a few months ago and their work wasn't up to Blue Tail's standards. They were more preoccupied with office gossip instead. I made the decision that was best for the company."

"All three workers, Miss Wolfe? As the CEO, your job is to act on behalf of the board's best interests," Frank said. "You can't go around hiring and firing staff as you please because of some idle office gossip. Three staff in one week is not acceptable."

"I own this company," Ava exclaimed. "Are you forgetting that? I've run four Top 100 businesses, so I know what I'm doing. Cutting staff costs will reduce expenditures and overheads in this slow market. We may be selling more magazines than ever before but sales are down compared to last year. I did what I thought was best for the company. I don't run around like the Mad Hatter, Frank. I care about the longevity of Blue Tail Media."

Frank's lips twitched. "Remember, Ava, the CEO is accountable to the board for the company's performance. Whether you like to admit it or not, your coupling with Elias Dorne saved us from ruin. But if Blue Tail goes down, you're going down with it."

~ ~ ~

Elias was waiting for Ava when she entered the restaurant at two o'clock. He sat in a corner booth underneath a beam of light, nursing a perspiring bottle of beer. He smiled when he saw her, scooting out of the booth to embrace her. He looked good and smelled even better. A faint five o'clock shadow dusted his jawline. His dark hair was clipped shorter.

"You're looking well," Ava said, slipping into the black leather booth. "Your new life agrees with you."

"Ava." Her name escaped his lips as a whisper. His shoulder brushed hers as he took a seat next to her. "We need to talk."

"Elias, I haven't seen you in a month. Can we have a moment to say hello?"

"We don't have time for pleasantries, Ava. I have some news."

A chill rushed through her body as a million possibilities circled in her mind. Was Daisy pregnant? Were they moving out of the state after the wedding? "What's wrong?"

"I was emailed these today." He dug in his pocket and tossed a handful of grainy photographs onto the table.

Ava inspected the photos with trembling hands, unsure of what to expect. The grainy images captured the moment they emerged from the shed after the storm, disheveled, partially undressed. Elias's face was clear as day, whereas her face was hidden from the photographer.

"Elias, if the public ever found out about this affair, Blue Tail Media will have another scandal on its hands. I will lose my job and reputation."

"You can't even see your face! Look at the photo. You can clearly tell that the man is me."

"I've been on enough TV screens and magazine covers for people to recognise who I am. I won't be able to keep my identity secret for long."

Elias shuffled the photos into his palm and pocketed them. "It's too late, Ava."

"What do you mean? Have they already been leaked?"

He nodded. "Do you remember Mike Cordon from *The Coastal Times*? He emailed me the images yesterday. They've already been published."

"WHAT!" Ava's cry attracted the stares of nearby diners. She sunk deeper into the booth, covering her face in her hands. "Oh my God. What are we going to do?"

Elias reached over and pulled her hands away. "There's a silver lining, Ava."

"What will that be?"

"The photographs have only been published in *The Coastal Times*. Their readership is limited to the coast only."

"Is that supposed to make me feel better?" Ava cried. "It doesn't take much for things to go viral these days. Did Mike say who sent them to him?"

"An anonymous source. It could be anyone, Ava. A guest or a staff member from the hotel could've seen us coming out of the shed."

"Or Daisy and Liam."

His lips formed into a bitter line. "Daisy doesn't know about the affair or what happened at Long River Valley. Are you sure it wasn't Liam?"

"I don't know. He's suspicious about us but I doubt he knows the truth."

"Can you check his phone?"

"How? I'm not involved with him, Elias. I don't see him every day."

He reached for her hands and squeezed them. "It's important we rule out our partners. A stranger is easier to condemn. I'll check Daisy's phone when I see her tonight if you can do the same with Liam."

"I don't feel comfortable about this. Anyway, it's too late. The images are out. I think we should just come clean to Daisy and Liam. We'll feel better for it."

"Are you forgetting that I'm getting married in six months? If I told Daisy I cheated on her, she'd leave me for sure."

"What do you want to do instead? Buy every single copy of *Coastal Times* and burn them? What's the point of checking emails and phones? The damage has been done."

"I need closure," Elias said. "If Daisy leaked the images to Mike, I have collateral to leave her. There's no point starting a life together built on lies."

"If she leaked them, then she knows about us already," Ava replied. "Why hasn't she confronted you yet? The seminar was a month ago."

"That's what scares me. Daisy's been a follower all her life. She's never been assertive or confrontational. These photos give her great leverage over me."

"Do you trust her?"

"I'm marrying her, aren't I?"

"Elias, I'm not going down this road again." Ava sighed in defeat. "Fine, I'll check Liam's phone over the weekend but I don't think snooping into my ex-husband's mobile will solve—" A wave of nausea overcame her and Ava pressed a hand to her stomach. "Oh, not again."

"Are you all right?" Elias asked.

"I've been feeling sick in the stomach lately. It's just stress."

"Have you been to the doctor?"

"I'll go this week." She laughed when Elias cocked his eyebrow at her. "I promise." She let out a calming breath until the unease in her gut had passed. "So what's your new job? I heard you were hired by an agency."

"I'm a senior copywriter for First Words Creative." He smirked. "Honestly, it doesn't pay as well as Blue Tail, but I have my own team of writers. The work-life balance is more user friendly too."

"You could've had all that with me."

His gaze shifted to the table unable to meet her eyes. "No, I couldn't have, Ava. You already knew that. You expect the world from your staff and it takes more than working like a beast to succeed under your management. You're a ruthless business woman and that's what I love—" He cleared his throat. "I'm happy where I am, but nothing can ever replace our time together, Ava."

To deflect the tears pushing behind her eyes, Ava ordered a drink from a passing waiter. What was she expecting meeting up with Elias? Reconciliation? A confession of his undying love? She was foolish to think this meeting was nothing more than a warning. A warning to stay away from him.

"How's the wedding planning going?" she asked. "I remember having so much fun trying on dresses, picking flowers, and eating cake samples."

Elias took a swig of his beer. "I'm leaving it all to Daisy. My only job is looking for a suit."

"Are you serious? It's your wedding too."

He shrugged. "All I know is that she's having fun shopping for the wedding with her bridesmaids and mother. I don't want to interfere with that. I just need to show up on the day."

Elias's detachment towards the wedding made Ava hopeful. His nonchalant attitude instilled the notion that what they shared was more than a fling. Maybe she had a chance. "I wish you all the best, Elias." She forced a smile. "I really do. Please send me photos of the big day. I would love to see them."

"Would you, really?" He leaned over and kissed her cheek, his lips lingering for a moment. "Move on, Ava. You deserve so much more than the shit I'm dragging you through." He thumbed away a tear from her cheek and she flinched at his touch. "Keep me updated on Liam. I want to douse this fire before it becomes too big to handle." He tossed some cash onto the table and walked out of the restaurant, leaving a gaping hole in his wake.

Chapter 17

When Ava appeared on Liam's doorstep dressed in a titillating low-cut dress and killer high heels, her desperation knocked back feminism one hundred years. She felt stupid and senseless bending to the needs of a man. Back in the day, she loved playing the seductress, using her body to tease and titillate Liam. But there was a reason why their marriage had ended and she felt being here only opened old wounds.

She knocked on the door and waited, shifting her weight from one foot to another. Her feet were already aching in the three-hundred-dollar heels. A light switched on in the foyer and Liam opened the door, holding a bottle of red wine.

"Ava, you made it. Come in." He pecked a kiss on her cheek as he stepped aside to let her in, spending a good few seconds admiring her figure in the dress. "You're looking good."

"I bought it for this very occasion." She did a twirl on the spot, allowing one moment of submission. She needed Liam to be soft like putty, easy to manipulate and mould. She closed the front door with her hip and followed him into the kitchen.

Two wineglasses sat next to an extravagant cheese platter, dips and vegetable sticks. "In the six years we were married, the only thing you cooked was burnt toast. Did you do this?"

He came up behind her, his hot breath tickling the back of her neck. "I was optimistic when you called wanting to have dinner. You and I have something special, Ava. We're unlike other people and that's why we've bonded mentally and sexually. A day doesn't go by where I've regretted signing the divorce papers."

She spun around to face him, planting her palms against his chest, almost in a consolatory gesture. "Let's take things slow. We're dining as friends, so no funny business, got it?"

"No sex?"

"None."

Liam frowned and poured the wine into a flute. "There'll be more alcohol coming tonight, I promise."

Ava rolled her eyes with a smile and carried the cheese platter and wineglass to the dining room. She sunk into the depths of the couch, catching sight of Liam's phone on the coffee table. With a small gasp of triumph, she cast a glance over her shoulder. Liam was neck deep in the fridge. There was no chance of checking it now without him catching her. What excuse would she use? She had to get as much liquor into her ex-husband as possible.

"What's for dinner?" she asked.

"Lamb shoulder and roasted veggies," Liam said proudly, sitting down next to her. "I slaved all day in the kitchen to impress you."

"Your sister was here, wasn't she?"

"How can you tell?"

Ava pointed to a woman's jacket draped over a bar stool. "That's Fiona's blazer. She lent it to me last winter. Liam, it's okay to admit it."

"Damn, I hoped you wouldn't notice." He tossed her a sideways smirk and took a sip of wine. "Fiona's a sous chef in the city so I called her over before she started work."

"I hope you paid her."

"See that bottle of red on the kitchen bench? I'd bought five bottles for dinner tonight. I gave her the rest as payment."

There was an air of desperation to Liam that Ava found charming. He was trying hard to impress her, to win her back. She felt a little guilty leading him on, but what would it matter if they slept together? She was single. He was single. There was no exclusivity with Elias. They didn't belong to one another. Besides, she missed the warmth of a man's body next to her.

She crossed one leg over the other, purposely showing off some thigh, and relaxed into the lounge. "How's business, Liam? Has your clientele increased since the fundraiser?"

"I guess so, but do we have to talk about work now?" Liam's brows knotted over a fixed gaze—the same kind of glare he used during their marriage. "This is dinner, not a business meeting."

"It was always business when we were married," Ava retorted. "We never talked about the weather or our favourite TV shows."

"We're not married anymore, Ava."

"I'm trying to make conversation because we're falling back into the same pattern. We don't know how to talk about anything else."

Liam cleared his throat. "You're right. Wasn't it the lack of communication that broke our marriage?"

"Among other things," Ava said dryly.

Liam finished his wine and got up to get a beer from the fridge. "I have one more thing to ask before we can move on."

"Go for it."

Ava's blood chilled when he returned with a copy of *The Coastal Times.* He opened it to the two-page spread of her and Elias. "Do you know who the woman is?" he asked, tossing her a glance. "She's the hottest topic in the office right now. My staff are putting bets on who it may be."

Ava couldn't tell if Liam was genuinely intrigued or was trying to trap her into admission. The mysterious woman had no discernible features and her hair was darkened from the rain. There were plenty of women at the seminar who matched the description.

"I don't know who she is," Ava lied.

"I don't remember Elias having a wandering eye," Liam said, observing the photos more closely. "Daisy was with him the entire weekend. He's got balls of steel to sneak off and bang another woman."

"I don't think it was intentional."

"You're condoning his actions after what happened between us?" Liam quizzed, placing his empty bottle beer on the table.

"Of course not. I was his employer, not his keeper. What he did in his spare time was his own business."

"So it is true," Liam said with a triumphant smirk. "Elias did quit his post. I didn't expect you to tell me right away, but I thought I was privy to some courtesy."

"Courtesy for what? We're not business partners anymore. You sold your share of Blue Tail, remember? I didn't have to tell you anything. I report to the board."

"How did they react to his resignation? I can't imagine it went down too well."

Ava dunk back her glass of wine. "They were fucking unimpressed, but it was too late to ask him back."

"Did he resign after the photos came out?"

"No, it was before that so I don't know his motives for leaving." Ava reached over and flipped the paper shut. "I thought he was happy."

"Did you ever find out who took the photographs?"

"Someone sold them to the media. He's lucky the circulation is only limited to the coast. If the pictures found a larger audience, it would ruin Elias's reputation."

"That's the thing about the media, honey." Liam patted her knee before climbing out of the sofa. "There are spies everywhere. Editors talk and soon enough pictures of Elias cheating on his missus will be posted all over the Internet. I wouldn't be surprised if someone close to him had done it. Why would a stranger care?"

Ava's motive to check Liam's phone became clearer. He had contacts in the press and his suspicions over her relationship with Elias had created ill will towards them. It wouldn't surprise her if Liam had leaked the images. His mobile sat at arm's reach, taunting her, and she hoped his pin number hadn't changed. Liam banged around in the kitchen as he prepared the rest of dinner. The rich, salty aroma filled the room, momentarily distracting her.

"The lamb smells incredible, Liam," she said, turning around in her seat, sniffing the air. "I can't remember the last time I cooked it."

"You don't cook, Ava. You get people to do it for you." Liam heaved the lamb rack onto the kitchen bench. "My sister is famous for her almond and spice crumb. The entire rack is covered in it."

"Can't wait to taste it."

"The meat needs to rest so I'll go for a piss." He pulled off the oven mitts, wiped his hands on his jeans, and dashed down the hall towards the bathroom. Ava waited a beat before leaping for the phone. She sighed with relief as it unlocked without hassle. Her ex-husband's pin code was still her birth year.

Ava scrolled through his images hastily, keeping one eye on the hallway. She ignored the porn screenshots of women's bits and uncovered images taken around the same time of the seminar. There was nothing incriminating, so she explored his deleted folder. *Zilch*. Ava's breath quickened in time with her racing heart, unable to think of an excuse if Liam caught her.

Panic clawed up the back of her throat at the sound of the toilet flushing. Frantically, she finished her search and almost tossed the phone in frustration when she couldn't find any evidence. She was foolish to think she would. Liam disliked the notion of his ex-wife with another man but she didn't think he would stoop so low.

Liam reappeared in the kitchen and withdrew a knife from the wooden block. "Have you spoken to Elias lately?" he asked nonchalantly.

"Are we going to talk about him all night?"

"No, I'm just curious because you two were pretty tight." Liam viciously carved into the meat in what Ava imagined was a small act of jealousy.

"Do I have to keep repeating myself? Elias was my employee. Nothing more. Nothing happened, Liam."

"Keep telling yourself that," he murmured. "There was always something there. I will get you to confess sooner or later." He glanced up, his dark eyes fixed on her. "Come and eat before the lamb gets cold."

~ ~ ~

"Ava, you're pregnant."

The air in the doctor's office appeared to thin as Ava sat in stunned silence. It felt like she was in a dream, weightless and helpless, grasping for stability. If she reached out, would someone be there to hold her down?

"Ms. Wolfe, are you all right?" The doctor leaned forward in his chair and gingerly touched her arm.

Ava jerked in her seat, crashing back down to earth. "I'm all right. Just a little stunned."

"It's okay to be shocked. You have a lot to process."

"That's an understatement."

Mal Tarvis turned to his computer and opened Ava's test results. "The pregnancy would explain the nausea and fatigue you've been experiencing lately."

Ava kneaded her temples with two fingers. "How far along am I?"

"Four weeks."

The pregnancy coincided perfectly with her liaison with Elias at the seminar. She assumed her missed period this month was due to stress. Ava felt the pressure of tears push behind her eyes. There were so many things running through her mind that she could hardly breathe. Short, ragged breaths escaped her lips, making her lightheaded.

"Judging by your reaction, I can only assume this baby wasn't planned," Mal said softly.

"No, it wasn't."

Mal leaned forward in his chair, his brow creased over his pale eyes. "Don't feel ashamed, Ava. I have many patients who are business women. They often find themselves with an unexpected pregnancy. It happens more frequently than you think."

"I'm always so careful. I'm on the pill."

"The contraceptive pill has a ninety-nine percent effective rate. There's always the one percent that slips through."

Ava covered her face with her hands, submitting to the darkness. She could hear the doctor's soft breathing, the mild chatter of patients in reception, and the ticking of his wall clock. Everything felt warped and unreal, like she was in a dream. If she removed her hands, would she wake up in bed?

"Ava, I have to ask my next question. Do you wish to continue this pregnancy?"

"I don't know."

Mal cleared his throat. "As a medical practitioner, I have my patient's wellbeing as my top priority. However, there are options if you decide termination is best for you."

A breath caught in Ava's chest and she released it gradually through narrowed lips. After a pregnancy scare at university, she vowed never to find herself in a doctor's office again, but the thought of aborting this child sickened her. "I want to have this baby."

Her confession came from the very depths of her soul, unwavering and real. It was frightening because Ava was never a maternal person. But at thirty-four years old, she wondered if time was running out to start a family.

"Do you have a husband or boyfriend?"

Ava shook her head ashamedly. "No, I'm single. The father is getting married to someone else and I can't bear to tell him. It will destroy his relationship."

"It's important that expecting single mothers have a solid support system behind them," Mal said. "Do you have one? Are you close to your family or friends?"

Ava's mother Veronica ceased all contact when she married Liam and she didn't have friends outside the business world. She abandoned everyone near and dear when she started working in the industry. Who needed friends when you had contacts and allies in business? "There's no one in my life I can rely on." The admission hurt, pained her to think she was alone.

Mal swivelled around in his chair and gathered some brochures from a drawer. "There are some wonderful supports groups in Sydney who help women in your situation."

"I'll look into them right away."

"Okay, good. I suggest getting onto prenatal vitamins such as folate as soon as you can. Eliminate all alcohol and cut back on coffee. It can stimulate the foetus."

"When will I start showing?"

"It's hard to say because this is your first pregnancy. Most mothers starting showing around twelve to sixteen weeks, so you have time to work out your wardrobe." He typed away on his keyboard. "I would like to see you in another four weeks to see how you're progressing. It's an exciting time, Ava. Please don't stress about the baby. Your maternal instincts will kick in soon."

"I'm not concerned about that. I work in a very male-dominated industry. I'm the CEO of a publishing company. I don't think the board will react well to the news."

"Ava, I've always told my patients to put their health first. Women get pregnant. It's only natural. This baby may be your redemption." Mal lowered his large hand over hers. "You need to slow down. I'm sure your employers will understand if your work load is eased. Saying that, I would really like you to find a support group. You may meet some like-minded women. Will you do that for me?"

Like a flip of a coin, Ava's life had irrevocably changed from a childless woman to an expectant mother. As a little girl, she had preferred playing with marbles, toy cars, and the neighbourhood boys. Dolls and girly things were foreign to her. As an adult, the companies she owned were like her children, growing and thriving under her care. But she was getting older and maybe this baby was her one chance of moving on with her life.

Chapter 18

"How many buttons, sir?" the tailor asked, unwinding the tape measure from his shoulders.

"Three, please," Elias replied.

"What about the trousers?"

"Tapered."

"Of course, sir. Very smart."

An hour later, Elias had left his suit fitting feeling a little violated. The tailor had poked and prodded every inch of his body that he should've bought the bloke dinner. There was something oddly intimate about a man running his fingers up another man's inner seam.

Overall, the suit was one more task ticked off his list. There was still so much to do: flowers, cake, honeymoon, groomsmen. In a way, he was grateful that Daisy had taken control over the planning so he could focus on work. It was the only thing that distracted him from thoughts of Ava. Memories of her often came with a side of guilt. At night, as he stared at the ceiling, sleepless, he wondered if he had time to call off the wedding. He loved Daisy, but there was always another woman consuming his thoughts.

Elias wandered the bustling city streets, looking for a bite to eat. The lunchtime crowd occupied the sidewalk like rolling waves, sucking him into the swell. The city offered a smorgasbord of foreign cuisine. The spicy aromas of Indian enticed him. The greasy scent of Chinese food seduced him. But Elias didn't feel like anything too heavy. He bought a sandwich and walked across the road towards the sun-drenched park. As he sat underneath the large canopy of a fig tree, his mobile vibrated in his pocket. Without looking at the caller ID, he answered, "Elias speaking."

"It's me."

He stilled, his sandwich hovering mid-air. "Ava." He cleared his throat. "How are you?"

"Did I catch you at a bad time?"

"No, I'm just having something to eat actually. How are you?"

"I've been better. Can I see you? We need to talk."

Something about her words froze his tongue to the roof of his mouth. Her emotionless voice set his heart racing. "What's wrong? Are you hurt?"

"Where are you?" she asked.

"Hyde Park. I'm sitting near the fountain."

"I'll be there in twenty minutes."

"You didn't answer my question. Are you okay?"

"You'll see when I get there." Ava hung up.

Elias couldn't eat another bite of his sandwich as he waited for Ava. She sounded different on the phone, impassive and emotionless, and he grew concerned over her wellbeing. He couldn't deny the past month must've been hard on her, losing grip of her control over him. He was free from her, but did he want to be?

A woman crossed the park towards him, her hips swaying lazily underneath her floral dress. She wore dark sunglasses and a wide brim hat, shielding locks of copper hair. Elias's heart quickened as she neared. It was Ava. He hadn't recognised her thicker waist or the slight slouch of her shoulders.

She embraced him without a greeting, burying her face in the nook of his neck. He wrapped his arms around her, a small part of him grateful to hold her again.

"Are you all right?" he whispered.

"I've missed you."

Unresponsive, he sat down on the bench and waited for her to join him. The air was thick with the sweet scent of her perfume. He bit down the urge to kiss her, to taste her rosebud lips again. Instead, he dug his nails into his palm, diverting the anguish into pain.

"Did you find out if Liam leaked the photos? Is that why you're here?"

She shook her head. "Liam didn't do it. I don't believe he leaked to the press. I couldn't find anything on his phone or email." She played with a stray thread on her dress. "Have you checked out Daisy?"

"I haven't had the time, Ava. In-between my crazy work schedule and organising the wedding, Daisy's asked me to plan the engagement party. These days, I rarely have time to scratch my own ass."

"When will the party be?"

"Not sure. Most venues need a six to eight-week notice period. It will probably be mid-year. Why you wanna know?"

"This will be the last time you see me, Elias." She removed her sunglasses slowly. Her emerald eyes were wide and fearful, tears threatening to fall. "You've changed my life. Somehow, you managed to break through this cold exterior of mine. Even Liam couldn't do that. We may have shared some intimate moments together but it was all an education."

"Ava, you're scaring me. What's going on?"

She swallowed hard and diverted her gaze to her stomach, rubbing it with one hand. "I'm pregnant."

If time had stopped at that very moment, Elias wouldn't have noticed. His entire body froze, his brain firing synapses as he went into shock. He gulped a breath of air and glanced at Ava, realising his reaction was probably not what she was expecting. Tears streamed down her pale cheeks.

"Say something, please," she pleaded.

"Is it . . . is it mine?" He forced the words from his lips, frightened of the answer.

She nodded. "Yes."

He ran a hand through his hair. "What are you going to do?"

"I've decided to keep it, if that's what you mean. Is that okay with you?"

Her question held an accusatory tone which he ignored. Elias swallowed the lump in his throat, his brain trying hard to put the pieces together. All he could think about was Daisy and the impeding heartache that would follow. "How far along are you?"

"Four weeks. Elias, the seminar was a month ago."

"Are you certain it's mine? You shared a room with Liam that weekend. Did you sleep with him?"

Ava's eyes shadowed with hurt. "The baby is yours You're just scared. That's all."

"Of course I am!" His booming voice attracted the stares of people picnicking nearby. He tried to reach for Ava, but she rebuffed his grasp. "Ava, I'm sorry. A baby doesn't fit into the schemes of things right now. I'm getting married."

"I'm not changing my mind," she insisted. "I'm keeping it. It may be my last chance to be a mother. Just be glad that I told you now. I could've waited until the baby was born."

"I'm not asking you to change your mind." Elias was almost whispering now. "I want the best for this child. Now, I have to somehow explain this to Daisy considering I cheated on her." He cleared his throat. "Have you told anyone else?"

"No, I have no one else, Elias. You're my entire world." She shook her head with self-doubt. "God, how did I end up like this? I'm in a high profile, well-paying job with the power to influence others. I have people cowering in fear when I enter the room, but this baby has turned me into a big sap. I am absolutely terrified of the future."

He took her hands and squeezed them. "It's normal to feel that way. I want to be a part of the baby's life, Ava, if you let me."

"What about Daisy? She and I are bound to bump into each other in the next eight months. I can't use the Liam card all the time."

Elias blew out a ball of air. "If I admit this baby is mine, she'll have the cause to leave me. Our affair will come to light and soon the entire country will hear about it. Daisy isn't the type of woman to let something slip under the rug, especially with the matters of her heart."

"It's probably a good thing you resigned when you did. The media can't say you quit when you found out about the baby."

"That's true but they'll do the math. I quit the same week we conceived. The press isn't stupid."

"What do you want to do?" Ava asked. "I don't want to add more stress to my life than I already have."

"Deny it."

"What?"

"Deny the baby's father. Plenty of famous women have done it through history. The father's identity is kept private and the public is none the wiser. We don't work together anymore and no one has discovered our affair. It might work, Ava."

"It might. Are you going to tell your mother? She's having a grandchild after all."

"I don't know yet."

"Does she like Daisy?"

A faint smile hooked the corners of Elias's lips. "To be honest, she liked you more. I can't predict how my mother will react when I tell her. I'm sure she'll keep it private, but family are usually the ones who accidentally leak things to the press."

"When do you see her next?"

"The engagement party." He turned to her. "I convinced Daisy to invite you."

The colour drained from Ava's face. "Is that a good idea? We were discussing keeping your identity private and now you want to go public. It will be suicide."

"I never said we'll go public, Ava. See it as a test. As far as everyone is concerned, you're just another friend invited to celebrate our engagement."

"When did you say the party was?"

"In about six weeks. Why?"

"I'll be ten weeks along by then. I'll be showing a little bump. People may notice."

Elias tenderly placed his hand on her belly, stroking it with the pad of his thumb. "I don't want you to think I'm ashamed of this baby. Because I'm not."

"It's not an ideal situation. You're getting married to another woman and I'm single. Society frowns upon women who have poor judgment of character."

Elias chuckled. "Ava, this isn't the 1950s." He reached over and gently cupped her cheek in his hand. His heart fluttered when she pressed into it. "I'll be with you every step of the way, I promise. You won't be alone. Ever."

~ ~ ~

The drive to Veronica's house outside of Sydney always took a toll on Ava. It unearthed memories and heartache she had long since buried. She couldn't remember the last time she saw her mother, years passing since they spoke. Veronica never ventured into the city to visit her, happy to remain in her dust ridden, fifty-year-old cottage. But circumstances had changed so it was time to mend old wounds.

Ava bit her inner cheek as she turned down the main road of Doveport. The small town had remained the same cesspool, unchanging in the last fifteen years. Debilitated brick buildings displayed rotting shop signs and dirty windows. Dogs ate rubbish in the gutters. Old, banged-up cars were parked outside the supermarket. Ava suspected her shiny black Mercedes must've looked like a mirage to the locals. Wealth was as rare as employment in Doveport and Ava had been lucky to leave town before the recession. Others weren't so lucky. Many residents, including Veronica, lost their livelihoods when stores closed down. Ava heard through a friend that her mother worked in a clothing store before it shut down. Due to her stubbornness, Veronica refused to leave town to find another job, so she spent most of her unemployment benefits on cigarettes and alcohol.

Ava drove on until she pulled into her old street. She slowed the car to a crawl, inspecting the old homes she remembered as a child. The same residences still stood, proudly displaying additional levels or renovated structures. Some had been cleared all together, leaving behind vacant lots. She turned the corner and spotted her childhood home cushioned between two brand-new brick mansions. It was an odd sight to see Veronica's little cottage eclipsed by the monstrosities, particularly since Doveport's housing market offered nothing for new home buyers.

Ava parked the car and closed the door behind her. The cottage looked smaller now, and more rundown since she last saw it. Overgrown vines curled around the veranda awning and the cobbled pathway was broken and misplaced from underground roots.

The cracked navy paint flaked under the strength of the sun rays.

Ava flicked a tear from her cheek. This wasn't the house she grew up in. It was a dump, and she dreaded meeting the creature living inside it.

She made her way to the front door and knocked. There was a scrape of chair legs against timber and someone walked to the entrance. Ava barely recognised her own mother as she drew gaze up and down Veronica's body. Veronica wore a pink dressing gown, emblazoned with a white bunny rabbit on the breast. Her fiery red hair was an unbrushed mess on top of her head. Her green eyes, once as vivid and beautiful as an emerald stone, were lifeless and dull.

"Hello, Mum."

Her mum's lips partially opened as if trying to comprehend the well-dressed woman in front of her. "Well, look at that. The prodigal daughter returns." Her voice was thick and harsh from years of smoking.

"I'm sorry for being here unannounced, but I wanted to see you. I have something to tell you." She cast a glance over her mother's shoulder. The hallway was too dark to see anything. "Can I come in?"

Veronica sniffed, studying her daughter with a critical eye. "I guess so. I'm about to sit down for lunch. Have you eaten?"

"I've only had coffee."

A faint sliver of motherly love flashed in her eyes. "Come on then. I'm about to make a sandwich."

Ava followed her mother inside, sidestepping towering piles of newspapers, random shoes without their partner, loose mail, and boxes of junk. The stench of mothballs and cigarette smoke lingered in the air.

"What would you like on your sandwich?" Veronica asked as she opened the fridge. "I have tomato, ham, cheese, and some salad." She glanced over her shoulder. "What about a coffee?"

"I don't need another cup, but a tomato and cheese sandwich sounds lovely." Ava hung by the dining table, one hand grasping the back of the chair. She couldn't believe this rundown shack used to be a beautiful Victorian house. Memories of sneaking her old boyfriends down the creaking hallway or reading a book under the frangipani tree in the backyard flooded her mind.

"Please sit down, Ava." Veronica wobbled to the kitchen bench with the sandwich ingredients and pulled a knife from the block. "Make yourself at home."

Ava obeyed, carefully shifting aside cigarette trays, tissue boxes, and piles of paper strewn across the table.

"I haven't had visitors in a long time," Veronica remarked. "In fact, you were the last person I was expecting to see on my doorstep. I haven't heard from you in years."

"I know, I'm sorry for that. Things were rough between us and I had to out of this town, get out of the toxicity. I was suffocating here."

"You could've called me anytime to let me know you were okay."

"Communication runs both ways, Mum," Ava replied. "It doesn't take much to pick up the phone or catch a train into town. I'm only ninety minutes away."

"It was your decision to turn your back, Ava," her mother retorted. "You never seemed to fit here. Doveport was always below you. Never good enough for you."

"Mum, I didn't come here to fight."

The corner of Veronica's lips upturned. "I'm just surprised to see you, that's all. Are you still working at that publishing joint?"

"I own Blue Tail Media. In fact, I own several businesses. I thought you knew this."

"I read about the Hayes scandal in the paper. Don't you think buying Blue Tail was a bad idea? Kinda like flogging a dead horse. There's no point." Veronica lowered her sandwich down in front of Ava.

"The point was to save it. I've done very well for myself buying failing companies and selling them at a profit. With my help, Blue Tail has regained its reputation and place at the top of the market. I'm very proud of what we've accomplished."

"What kind of money do you make now?" Veronica sat down opposite her, biting off the corner of her sandwich.

Ava chewed at her bottom lip, already anticipating the money questions. While she was happy to lend her mother some cash, Ava had learned over the years that money meant more to Veronica than her own daughter. "Enough to keep me going."

"You obviously make enough to buy that shiny Mercedes outside." The distaste in Veronica's voice dripped from her lips. She reached for a bottle of vodka on the table and poured herself a glass. "How's Liam these days?"

Ava cleared her throat, trying her hardest to keep her food down. She wasn't aware that morning sickness could debilitate a woman the entire day. "He's fine, I guess. I don't see him every often these days."

"Do you still sleep with him?" When Ava made a noise of protest, Veronica continued with a hint of triumph. "I remember you couldn't keep your hands off him when you were divorcing. That's what Jennifer told me, anyway."

"You're friends with Liam's mother?"

Veronica lifted a shoulder. "We talk now and again on Facebook. I speak to her more than I do with you."

Ava sighed and tossed her sandwich onto the plate. "Mum, I didn't come here to fight. I have something to tell you. I hope you'll remain civil about it."

"You're getting married again?"

"No."

"Are you pregnant?"

Ava smiled weakly as Veronica's eyes widened. She pushed her plate away, needing the space to slap the table. "I knew it! I thought you looked a bit thicker around the waist. Do you have a boyfriend?"

"No." Ava's cheeks flushed red. She couldn't understand why she felt like a little girl again in her mother's presence.

"Oh, so you slept with some random bloke and he knocked you up."

"It's not like that."

"Do you know who the father is?"

"I do, but I rather not say."

Veronica reached across the table for her hands, her face feigning pity. "Honey, I'm your mother. You can tell me anything. To be honest, I'm surprised you weren't knocked up as a teenager. You used to run around like the town's bicycle, screwing all the—"

Ava jerked her hands free and pushed her chair back. "I asked you to be civil and your attitude is exactly what I wanted to avoid. You're my mother. You should be on my side, not belittling me by calling me a slut."

Veronica stood up and rounded the table towards her. "Okay, you're right. I'm sorry. It's just hard for me to adjust. You turn up on my door eighteen years later with a flashy car and a pregnant belly. You're carrying my first grandchild. I didn't mean for any bad blood."

"There's always bad blood between us, Mum. From the moment I was born, you and I always butted heads over clothes, makeup, and men. Do you remember stealing my first boyfriend when I was seventeen? From memory, you took him away on the night of our first date and fucked him in my own bed! You couldn't understand why I didn't speak to you for a month." Ava brushed tears from her eyes. "Your attitude towards men imprinted on me like a tattoo. When I became an adult, I used my sexuality like currency. I used my body to get the things I wanted. I bedded men for their money or power and discarded them like trash—just like you used to do. Like mother, like daughter, hey?" She glanced down and stroked her belly lovingly. "But things will change for this baby. I came here to mend fences. I want you to be a part of your grandchild's life."

Her mother's eyes filled with tears when she bought Ava in for an embrace. "I would really love that, Ava. I'm sorry for the way I treated you as a child. It was selfish to put my needs first. When your father left, I lost a piece of myself and I took it out on you. But I won't be making the same mistakes with my grandbaby."

The two women clung to each other as they cried, releasing years of built-up anger and pain. Ava had missed having her mother close, someone familiar and constant.

"What would you say about moving in with me?" Ava proposed. "I have a five-bedroom house so I have plenty of space. You can help me raise this baby. I want my mother back in my life again. What do you think?"

Veronica cast her gaze around the cluttered living room and Ava saw sadness bloom in her eyes. "Mum, we can renovate this place and sell it," she said, taking her hand. "The money can help you rebuild a better life outside of Doveport. This town is eating away at you. I can help you get a job in the city and eventually buy a new house. It will give you a chance to move on."

"I don't know if I can do that, Ava."

"Mum. I want this to work. But in order for us to achieve this, I need to know you've changed. I need to know if you are willing to put your past, this house behind you."

Her mother shook her head with self-doubt. "When you moved away, you created a very successful life. Not many people can do that. Besides, I have so many memories of your childhood in this house." She stroked her daughter's cheek. "I'm so happy we were able to reconcile for the baby, but I'm not ready to leave my home."

Ava knew it would be a tough sell so she propped her handbag on the table and pulled out a key. Pushing it into her mother's hand, she said, "This is the spare key to my house. You are welcome to stay anytime. There's still a while before this baby arrives so you have time to think about." She grabbed her mother's hand and placed it across her belly. "I need you, Mum. We need you. You're all we have in this world."

Chapter 19

Elias couldn't shake the feeling of impending doom. The engagement party was in full swing and Ava was nowhere to be seen. He wasn't surprised. She'd accepted the invitation out of politeness and dropped off the radar. There was no mention of attending prenatal scans with her or going pram shopping together. The only gesture she made was buying an early engagement party gift—an expensive China dinnerware set that was delivered to his unit.

There was no denying he missed her. Ever since he quit Blue Tail, he'd left a part of himself behind. There was a unique bond formed between he and Ava, a partnership an outside party would think was strange. Dependable. Reliant.

But their union had created something special. He tracked every week like clockwork, downloading pregnancy apps on his phone so he could keep up with the baby's progression. He had to be careful around Daisy, but she was so caught up with wedding planning that she hadn't noticed her fiancé chatting to fathers on online forums. He wanted to be a good parent to this child. It meant more to him than anything else.

Two arms wrapped around his middle and someone's hot breath tickled his ear. "Lisa, how many times do I have to tell you? I'm getting married."

"I'll find Lisa and I'll kill her." Daisy stood behind him, hands planted on her hips. Her red lips were pulled into a pout.

"Daisy, I'm only kidding."

"Oh." The pout was replaced with a dazzling smile. She

sidled up to him, resting her head on his shoulder. "Are you having fun so far?"

The venue for the engagement party was held at an old community hall, adorned with pink and white streamers hanging from the ceiling, a kitchen full of food and chairs embellished with pink ribbon. Forty people were invited to the party, happily chatting around the room, drinking punch and gossiping. Most of the guests were Daisy's friends and family, so he was outnumbered.

"It's great," he said. "I think people are enjoying themselves."

"Do you have anyone else coming from your side?"

"Yes, Ava was supposed to come. Maybe she's caught up."

"Oh, it doesn't matter if she can't make it. I'll keep a slice of cake for her just in case."

"She's not coming," Elias replied flatly.

"I know." Elias extracted himself from Daisy's embrace and wandered to the punch bowl. It was non-alcoholic, but if he was going to survive this party, he needed something stronger. A hush settled over the crowd as the church doors opened. A woman entered the room slowly, her high heels tapping against the timber floor. It was Ava. Elias dropped his plastic cup and approached her. She wore a loose-fitting dress that concealed the tiny baby bump. He bit down the urge to run his hand over her belly, knowing he was being watched by forty sets of eyes.

"You made it," he said, taking the coat she shrugged off her shoulders. "Did you find the place okay?"

"Yes, it's pretty easy once you get onto the main road."

They remained civil as he escorted her across the room, his hand placed protectively on the small of her back. They approached Daisy standing with some friends and Elias felt Ava's body stiffen as they neared.

"She won't bite," he whispered in her ear.

"Her friends might."

Daisy opened her arms and pulled Ava into an awkward embrace. "Thank you so much for coming and the dinnerware set was absolutely gorgeous. You shouldn't have!"

"No problem at all. It will last for years."

Daisy inspected Ava's dress with a judgmental eye, fingering the lace motif around her collar. "This is nice. Designer?"

Ava nodded. "Zac Posen, last season."

"Oh, I love his designs. They're so feminine."

"He's a friend of friend actually," Ava said. "If I'm lucky, I get his garments half price."

Daisy's girlfriends responded in a chorus of "oohs" and "ahhs" and bombarded Ava with questions about her mysterious friend. Elias watched the conversation with a combination of amusement and dread. Ava handled the interest with poise and grace, used to having a thousand questions thrown at her. But Daisy hated having the attention diverted away from her. She stood next to Elias, arms crossed defiantly over her chest.

"I thought it was a bad idea inviting her," she whined, pouting.

"Why?"

"It's my engagement party. It's supposed to be about me."

"Excuse me, Daisy. It's my party too," Elias argued. "Stop acting so spoiled. Ava's trying to be friendly. It's hard being in a room full of strangers."

"Isn't that her job? She should be used to talking to people." Without another word, Daisy spun on her heels and marched towards her parents standing in the corner of the hall. Her friends scuttled off once they realised she was gone.

Elias let out a breath of air as Daisy shot daggers at him from across the room. "I'm sorry you had to witness that."

"Daisy doesn't like me," Ava said.

"I don't think she ever will."

"I should go. I don't think it's wise my being here." She hooked her handbag over her shoulder and turned to leave.

"Wait." Elias grabbed her arm and pulled her back, unintentionally crashing her body against his. They stared at each other as the entire room stilled. Sparks sizzled in the air between them and Elias realised he was still holding onto Ava's arm. God, he wanted to kiss her. He wanted to drown in those emerald pools. "If you want to leave," he said, "I won't stop you."

Her lips pulled into a sneer. "Everyone is looking at me like I'm wearing some scarlet letter. What has Daisy told them about me?"

"She's just jealous. Ignore her."

"It was a bad idea coming. I should leave, Elias."

His name spilling from her sweet lips was all he needed to hear. He escorted her through the hall and out to her Mercedes. Luckily, she had parked down the street so no one could see him push her against the car. Despite a small noise of protest, Ava welcomed his kiss, folding into him like a puzzle piece. She tasted so sweet and warm. He brushed his fingertips along the curve of her jaw. "I missed you so much," he purred between kisses. "I'm glad you came today. It's nice to see your belly's getting bigger."

Ava stilled and broke the kiss. "We shouldn't be doing this, Elias. It's your engagement party, for Christ's sake."

"I want *you*, Ava. It was foolish of me to propose to Daisy when you're carrying my baby."

She planted her hands firmly on his cheeks and stared into his eyes. "No, you'll go through with this wedding. You've committed to Daisy. You love her. You don't love me." She blinked back tears. "You and I were never meant to be together."

He shook his head, caressing her belly lovingly. "If we weren't meant to be together, how did we create this miracle?"

Ava leaned forward and pressed a lingering kiss on his cheek. "Go back to Daisy, Elias. She'll be wondering where you are." She opened the car door, putting one foot in. "I'll be in touch. Good luck, Elias."

When he returned to the hall, sombre, Elias's mother Karen was waiting for him by the front door. "You shouldn't be kissing another woman so close to your wedding," she said, handing him a plate of food.

"You saw that?"

"Yes, every second of it. Was that Ava Wolfe?"

Elias cast his gaze downwards, unable to look his mother in the eye. "Yes. I invited her."

"She'll break your heart, my darling boy," his mother said, cupping his cheek. "She will use you. You have a wonderful woman waiting for you in that hall. Your life with Daisy is about to begin."

"I thought you liked Ava?"

"I don't know her well enough to make an assumption. I only know what's best for my son. It's easy to be swept up by Ava's beauty and power. She's made a reputation on such skills. But there's no future with her, Elias. She's a businesswoman, married to the job. Her husband will always come second."

"Mum, there's something I need to tell you."

Karen looped her arm through his and dragged him towards the hall. "You can tell me inside. You have a cake to cut with your future bride."

"I don't think what I have to say is appropriate for all ears."

~ ~ ~

Ava dreaded the drive into work on Monday morning. She planned to disclose her pregnancy to the board. She was almost three months along and could no longer hide her growing stomach behind trench coats and scarves.

It frightened her to think how they would react, since more than half of the members were men. They didn't understand her situation, nor cared for it. Ava had spent half the night gazing up at the ceiling, thinking of possible ways to introduce her pregnancy and none of them seemed right. It would just have to come natural.

She found a parking spot outside a popular café in the city and wandered inside, eager to feed her pregnancy cravings. A juice and a chocolate chip muffin would do nicely.

She gave her order to the register clerk and took a seat in a booth as she waited. Judging by the people around her doing the same, she was in for a wait. To occupy herself, Ava reached for a newspaper on the stand next to her.

She let out an audible gasp at the blazing headline on the front page: PICTURE EXCLUSIVE: PUBLISHING GIANT CEO AVA WOLFE PREGNANT, SAYS SOURCE

Ava grabbed the copy before anyone could take it and read the article with trembling hands. The front page was splashed with a photo of her and Elias at the park. The photographer had captured a tender moment between Elias and Ava, gazing into each other's eyes. Unlike the leaked photos of the shed incident, Ava's face was clear as day.

A wave of nausea overcame her and she dashed out of the café. She turned into an alleyway and threw up in a trash can. There was no hiding now. Uncaring about her juice and muffin, Ava cleaned herself up and returned to the car. Her entire body shook violently and it felt like everyone who walked by was judging her.

Ava started the engine and drove into work. The board was waiting for her when she stepped off the elevator. Ignoring the inquisitive stares of her employees, she walked straight into the boardroom and closed the door behind her.

Chairman Frank Boulder sat at the head of the table as usual. But this time, he was only accompanied by the company's solicitor Henry Brooks. In front of him was a copy of the newspaper she saw at the café.

"Ava, please take a seat," Frank said, putting out his hand. "We would like to begin right away."

She pulled out a chair and sat opposite Henry. He looked like the stereotypical lawyer with his faultless suit, wire-rim glasses, and beady eyes. His lips thinned as he locked eyes with her.

"Frank, what's this about?"

Frank leaned forward in his chair, locking his fingers together. "Ava, do you remember the Bobby Hayes scandal?"

"Of course I do. It almost destroyed this company. But we rebuilt. The stocks prove our durability."

"You're right. You see, most large companies have the strength to survive one big scandal. That's it. If it doesn't destroy them, it means they have stability and security. But if it happens to be rocked by another one, consumers begin to question the business's ideologies and objectives. I don't want to lose Blue Tail Media after everything it's been through." He cleared his throat and looked at Ava right in the eye. "Did you have a sexual relationship with Elias Dorne during his employment?"

"I don't see how that's any of your business."

Frank flew to his feet so fast his chair rocketed into the wall behind him. "It is my business when my CEO is sleeping with one of her directors!" He leaned across the table and tossed the newspaper at her. "Is this article true? Are you pregnant with Dorne's baby?"

Ava swallowed hard and picked up the paper, skimming over the article.

Blue Tail Media CEO Ava Wolfe is reportedly pregnant with her first child. At the time of printing, she has not publicly come forward to announce the pregnancy or reveal the identity of the father. Wolfe was previously married to

PR expert Liam Heathcote for six years. He has denied any comment.

"What makes you think Elias is the father?" she asked.

"I haven't been blind to how close you two became during his employment," Frank said. "The late nights cooped up in your office, the multiple travel commitments and whispers behind closed doors. While I'm not one for office gossip, I couldn't ignore the rumours of your relationship outside of this building. Ava, I'm not trying to be the bad guy here. As you understand, we only want the best for this company."

"It's my business—"

"And I have the authority and power to overthrow you. I don't want that to happen." He sighed. "When were you going to tell us about the baby?"

Ava bit at her bottom lip until she tasted blood. There was no point denying it now. After all these years working in the media, it had turned its back on her. "Legally, I don't have to disclose to my employer until a month before my due date. I was going to tell you, Frank. Coincidentally, I planned on telling you this morning."

"Elias's resignation was not related to the pregnancy?"

"I don't know. I'm telling the truth, Frank. Elias left the company before both of us found out."

"Ava, I cannot risk another scandal rocking Blue Tail. We're still picking up the pieces from Hayes. Unfortunately, it looks like the media has already gotten whiff of it." He exchanged glances with Henry, who pushed a piece of paper in front of her. "We ask for you to step down from your role as CEO."

"Hell no! This company is my life," Ava argued, pushing the paper aside without reading it. "I'm not giving it up for some hefty payout. I can sue you for unlawful dismissal."

"I don't see any other way of making this disappear, Ava."

"I don't want this to go away, Frank. I'm a pregnant single woman. You'll just have to get used to it. Elias doesn't work for Blue Tail anymore, so what's the harm? This baby has nothing to do with the company. If anything, it will destroy my reputation, not Blue Tail's." She pushed back her chair and stood up, glaring at both men. "Don't take my threat of a lawsuit lightly, because if this conversation gets out, I will take it further."

Ava turned and exited the boardroom, heading straight for the elevators. She didn't wish to stay in the office for a minute longer. When she pulled into her driveway twenty minutes later, she recognised Liam's car parked on the street.

He was waiting for her at the front door, his leg cocked against the wall, his eyes shielded by dark aviator sunglasses. A newspaper was cradled underneath his arm. Ava groaned when she saw it, wondering if she would ever get through today without seeing another copy.

"Is it true?" Liam asked as Ava unlocked the front door.

"Is what true?"

Liam unwound the paper in her face and pointed at the front page. "Is the baby mine?"

"Liam, we haven't had sex in three and a half months." She tossed her keys and handbag onto the kitchen bench and flopped into the lounge, kicking off her shoes. "It's not yours."

"I've read the paper and seen the news. It's Elias's child, isn't it?"

"None of your business."

He perched his hands on his hips, lingering over her. "Elias seems to be the media darling at the moment, appearing in every bloody newspaper. That's him on the front page with his hand on your belly. I'm not an idiot, Ava."

"I'm not saying a word."

Then a light of recognition dawned on Liam's face and he took a few stumbling steps backwards. "He's your lover," he announced with an expression of awe. "You were the girl he was caught coming out of the shed with. Oh my God. It's all making sense now."

"So you didn't leak the photographs to Mike Corden?"

"Fuck no. That was Daisy."

Ava sat up razor straight on the lounge. "What did you say?"

"Daisy knew all along you were boning Elias at the seminar. She leaked the photos at Long River Valley and I'm pretty sure she's responsible for what's splashed across Monday's paper."

"She told you this?"

Liam sat down next to her. "Yes, she and I bonded during the seminar. She told me everything. She'd been suspicious of your relationship with Elias since he started working with you. She never wanted him to work for you in the first place. When the storm hit and you guys were nowhere to be found, she arranged the search party, so she could catch you in the act."

"I have to tell him!" Ava reached for her phone, but Liam intercepted her.

"You cannot tell him about Daisy."

"Why not? They're getting married so he deserves to know. They'll be starting their marriage on a lie."

"She asked me to keep it secret and I've already betrayed her trust." Liam brushed his hair off his forehead, exhaling. "I can't stop you from telling Elias. But it won't make him come back to you. He has too much to lose now. His job, his reputation. His woman."

"Daisy needs retribution. She accepted his marriage proposal for God's sake!"

"Right after you screwed him too, yes?" Liam said with a glint in his eye. "By accepting his proposal, Daisy has won over you. That's all she ever wanted. To have her man back under her control."

"She hasn't said anything to me."

"Why would she? You're the other woman. Leaking the photos was her way of publicly shaming Elias. It will destroy his reputation and force him to leave the industry. She's not just a dumb blonde, Ava. She has a very strategic mind."

"He still loves me, Liam. I know it. If he cares about me, he'll leave her. I'm carrying his baby, after all."

"Are you sure about that? History is full of unfaithful men who impregnated their mistresses, but remained married to their wives. Daisy will not let Elias go without a fight."

Ava chewed at her bottom lip. "Whose side are you on?"

Liam kicked off his shoes and threw his arms across the back of the couch. "I'm still on the fence with that one. You cheated on me multiple times during our marriage. If I remember correctly, you slept with a coworker in your office while I waited in reception. A leopard doesn't change its spots, Ava. What makes you think you won't fall into the same pattern if you and Elias end up together? A baby doesn't fix anything. Sometimes, it can make matters worse."

"So what you're saying is that I'm screwed either way."

He reached over and squeezed her hand. "I still care about you, Ava. I always will. But you have to admit that it's not the most ideal situation. Does the board know about the baby?"

"I had a meeting with Frank Boulder this morning. They are forcing me to resign. They don't want another Hayes scandal on their hands because, they believe, Blue Tail won't survive the downfall. But it's my company. I can't abandon it after I worked so hard in keeping its heart beating."

"Maybe it's for the best. You'll be giving birth in six months' time and I don't think I've ever known you to take a holiday. It's time for a break, Ava. You deserve it."

Ava stroked her belly as she gazed around her multimillion-dollar mansion. Money was always the driving force in her life. She had to have the biggest house, the expensive car, the designer wardrobe, but this baby forced her to redefine what life was all about. Love. Family. Unity. Her CEO salary was more extravagant than most, so she had plenty of savings in the bank to keep her going. Maybe it was time to downsize and reevaluate things. She could take a year off after the baby was born and think about going back to work when she was ready.

"So what are you going to do?" Liam asked.

"I think I need to make the right decision for my family."

Chapter 20

The library held a certain chill that Ava couldn't shake. It buried deep into her bones, feeling more like an omen than air conditioning. After putting it off for weeks, she decided to attend a support group for single mothers. The only one she could find close to the office was the local library. There was something shameful about admitting to her problems, but it would be good to speak to other women in the same situation. She might make some friends.

Ava approached reception, inconspicuously searching the library for other pregnant women. She spotted a few mingling between the aisles. A middle-aged woman behind reception stopped typing and surveyed her over thick black frames.

"Can I help you?"

"Yes, my name is Ava. I'm here to attend the support group."

A kindness came to her eyes. "Of course, my dear. Head towards the back of the library and look for Door 120. That's where the meeting's being held."

"Thank you." Ava turned to leave.

"Oh honey, wait," the woman called after her. "There's somebody here waiting for you. I've asked them to sit outside the room."

Ava turned and headed towards Door 120 with a bounce in her step. Who could be here to support her? Elias didn't know about the support group nor did Liam. When Ava caught sight of her mother sitting outside the room she started to cry.

"Mum, how did you know I was here?" She welcomed Veronica into a tight hug. Her hair was freshly brushed and coloured and she wore a brand-new orange cardigan.

"Your secretary told me you were at the library," she said. "I was hoping to catch you in time." She stroked Ava's belly, a small smile on her lips. "When do you go for the morphology scan?"

"In about seven weeks. I'll found out if I'm having a boy or a girl."

"What are you hoping for?"

Ava smiled. "I don't care as long as my child is healthy."

They entered the room and took a seat inside the circle of chairs. Other women had already arrived, talking amicably to each other. They were from all walks of life—big, small, rich and poor. Ava felt immediate comfort in their presence. They were all going through the same thing.

The counsellor arrived and took her place at the front of the room. She was a young woman with a bright, round, friendly face. "Ladies, my name is Emilia and welcome to the group. I want to start by saying this is a safe place. There will be no judgment or gossip here. We are sisters bound together by love for our children." She gazed around the room. "Let's go around the circle and introduce yourself. If you don't feel comfortable, you can only disclose your first name." Her eyes settled onto Ava. "Why don't we start with you?"

Ava grabbed her mother's hand and squeezed it. "My name is Ava, and this is my mother, Veronica."

"Welcome ladies," Emilia said. "Is this your first support group?"

"Yes."

"Don't be ashamed by being here, Ava. You are taking the next step in bettering your life for your child. We all are. Would you like to tell us what bought you here?"

Ava gripped onto her mother's hand tightly. Veronica didn't even flinch when her nails dug into her flesh. "I work for a well-known media publishing company in the city. I've always worked hard, never stopped to consider children in my future. I'm a divorcee and currently single. I'm not with the father."

"Have you told him about the baby?"

"Yes."

"Does he accept it?"

Ava smiled warmly at the memory of Elias's hand on her belly. "Very much so."

A chorus of cheers broke out around the circle.

"That's wonderful news, Ava," Emilia said. "It does make the situation easier when both parties are on the same path. Do you think you'll ever reconcile with the father?"

"No, he's getting married to someone else. My chance for a future with him is over."

"Having a child is all about rebirth, Ava," Emilia said. "Think of this time as a chance to grow and move on from the obstacles of your life. You are a mother now."

The support group continued for an hour as the other women shared their stories. Tearful, Ava sat in awe, listening to their plights. Some had left abusive relationships. Two women in the circle had been raped and considered suicide to end their suffering. She had what these women didn't: financial support, family, and a friendly relationship with the father.

When it was time to go, Ava gathered her things and handed them to Veronica. "Please wait for me," she said. "I'll be back soon."

"Where are you going?"

"I need to speak to Emilia."

She found her packing up the chairs, storing them in the corner of the room. She smiled as Ava approached. "Ava, I appreciate you finding the courage to attend today. I hope you were able to learn some things about yourself this afternoon."

"I did. Though, I was more touched by the other women in the room. I thought my situation was difficult, but these ladies are experiencing things I never dreamed of."

"That's why we have this group, so there's a safe place for women to go without judgement."

"I would like to help if I can."

Emilia's eyebrows snapped together. "How?"

Ava extracted her cheque book from her purse, scribbled an amount, and handed it Emilia.

The counsellor's eyes widened in shock. "Ava, I can't accept this."

"It's not much, but I hope my donation can help provide a safer location, food baskets, or a night at a hotel if the women need it. They've touched my heart, all of them."

Emilia's mouth was still open. "This is very generous of you. Twenty thousand dollars is too much." She pulled Ava into an embrace. "I can't thank you enough. The girls will be so happy. I see great things for you, honey. Great things. Please come back again."

As Ava walked back to her car with Veronica, she hoped Emilia's prophecy would come true. She deserved it.

~ ~ ~

"I think we should move in together," Daisy purred.

"Come again?" Elias stopped slicing the carrots and turned to her. Daisy's eyes were bright and optimistic. "I thought you wanted to wait until we were married."

"I practically live here so we're already living in sin."

"What do you parents think about it?"

Daisy picked up a spoon and dunk it into the sauce sizzling on the stove top. "I haven't told them yet. I'm a grown woman. I can make my own decisions." She tasted Elias's creation with relish before tossing the empty spoon into the sink. "Besides, I wanted to be out of the house before I get too old. I'm twenty-seven and still living at home."

"Your sisters moved out to live on campus or overseas, Daisy. It's different. My unit is an hour drive from your folks. Your mother freaked out when her eldest daughter moved to another suburb. How do you think she'll react when you tell her you want to move in?"

Daisy pouted her lips like a spoiled teenager. "Why do you keep avoiding the subject, Elias? I get the impression that don't you want us to live together."

"I still do, Daisy. There's so much going on with the wedding and work that my mind is struggling to keep up. I need time to adjust."

"You've had three months to think about it."

"I need more time," Elias insisted, returning to his cooking, unable to look Daisy in the eye. "We have six months until the wedding. Let's focus on planning instead."

"All right, let's talk about the seating charts then." Daisy extracted the list of guests from her purse and laid it out in front of her. "We've agreed to invite eighty-six guests, but I'm still waiting on your side. We have your immediate family, but what about friends or coworkers?"

Elias didn't know anyone well enough at First Words Creative to ask, and he rarely spoke to his friends anymore. There was only one person he wanted to come—not to humiliate or ridicule—but so he could see her again. Ava was under his skin, in his blood. He lived and breathed thinking of her and their unborn child. There was no way Daisy would send her an invitation. She was too insecure, wanting all the attention on her big day.

"So who do you want come?" Daisy pressed. "I have to give the venue the guest list by next Tuesday."

"I don't have as many friends or family as you do," Elias remarked, feeling a little hurt by her insistence. "I'll give you my list this week, I promise."

Daisy stared at him, unblinking. "Fine. Email it to me." She turned and wandered towards the living room. On her way, she passed the dining room table where Monday's paper was sitting unread.

To distract himself, Elias picked it up and unrolled it, almost gagging when he read the headline. **PICTURE EXCLUSIVE: PUBLISHING GIANT CEO AVA WOLFE PREGNANT, SAYS SOURCE**

His mind circled like a hurricane as he steadied himself against the table. Who was the source? The accompanying photo of his hand on Ava's belly looked like it was snapped on a mobile. It was poor quality, but there was no denying who the couple was.

He reached for his mobile to contact Ava before stopping himself. They had taken a risk meeting at the park and even a bigger risk showing affection in public. The source could've been anyone; a stranger misinterpreting their conversation or someone in Elias's circle.

He tossed the newspaper into the bin when Daisy returned to the kitchen to check on dinner. He'd seen a great change in her personality over the last few months. The timid little mouse had turned into a fierce lioness—protective, envious, bitter, and yet, still insecure. He had no evidence to prove Daisy was the leak, though it wouldn't surprise him. He deserved it after what he'd put her through.

"Dinner's about twenty minutes away," Daisy announced, draining the carrots into a colander. "The roast is still raw in the middle."

Elias headed for his bedroom down the hall. "I'm going for a run then. I'll be back soon." Not waiting for a response, he dressed into shorts and a T-shirt and pocketed his mobile.

He inhaled the brisk evening air deep into his lungs as he walked out of his apartment complex. The moon hung high in the sky, concealed by a whisper of silver clouds. Bats soared across the blackness, screeching. The city streets were deserted.

He took out his phone and dialled Ava. She answered after the second ring, her voice thick with consternation.

"Elias, is everything all right?"

"I read Monday's paper."

Her end went silent for a moment. "I saw it too. I can't believe someone's betrayed us."

"Do you know who?"

"I was going to ask you the same thing," she said. "This is the second time we've been outed. It's almost becoming a vendetta."

"I know of two people who are against our relationship."

"Liam and Daisy."

"Of course, they're the scorned lovers," Elias said. "Why would a member of the public care about us? I'm more concerned about how this is going to escalate. I can lose my job if my employer finds out."

"Hasn't it escalated already? The public knows I'm pregnant."

"But they don't know I'm the father. Some people think it's Liam."

"Can I see you?" Ava pressed. "There's something I need to tell you."

"I would love to see you, Ava, but it's not wise. Daisy's staying over tonight. Maybe another time."

There was hesitation in her voice. "There won't be another time, Elias."

Panic laced through his chest. "Why?"

"I'm stepping down from Blue Tail and leaving the city. There's nothing for me here, Elias. It seems every move I make is being captured. The last thing I want is to have your identity released. It will be best if I leave."

Elias joined the bustling dinner crowd on the street. Bright lights spilled onto the pavement, marking his path. "Where will you go?"

"I'm going to rent my house out and buy something smaller up north. I need to get away from the jeering eyes. I can't deal with the media anymore."

"Did the board kick you out?"

"They offered me a generous resignation package. Frank Boulder will take control of the company until they hire a replacement."

"Are you willing to give up Blue Tail so easily after everything you did for it? You fought so hard to reclaim it and now you're walking away."

"I'm doing it for us," Ava said. "I'm doing it for our baby. There's so much negativity in our lives right now, from our lovers' jealousy to the media's interest. I promise I won't be gone for long. I'll call you when I have settled so you can visit."

Elias slowed his pace, his gaze downcast, saddened. "Will you let me know when you have the baby?"

"Of course. I will send you as many photos and videos as I can without arousing Daisy's curiosity."

"I would like to help with child support."

Ava chuckled. "There's no need, Elias. I can support us perfectly fine." There was rustling on her end and he assumed she'd grabbed a tissue. "Good luck with everything in your life, Elias. I wish you all the best with your marriage. We will speak again soon."

"Ava, I love—" Before he could finish his sentence, she severed the call.

Chapter 21

Ava replayed the recorded footage of her press conference for the seventh time. Sipping her chai tea, she observed her television appearance with a critical eye, frowning at the choice of clothes she wore, how her hair was dressed, and the large swell of her swollen breasts. No one would take her resignation seriously now. They were so large that they knocked the lectern twice.

For three weeks, Ava had been working happily as an editor for *The Advocate* when Frank Boulder rang one day, insisting a press conference was needed urgently. The media had heard about her shock resignation and wanted answers. Now. Besides, Frank hoped the public appearance would appease the panicked stockholders threatening to pull.

Ava let Frank stew for a few days as she considered his plea. She didn't want to go back to Sydney after leaving everything behind. Especially Elias. His face was a constant fog in her memory. But her office was hounded by unsolicited press calls every day, even when she'd kept her new job out of the media. To clear the waters and Frank's conscience, Ava drove down to the city, conducted the press conference, and was back before lunch. There was no time for socialising. In and Out.

Ava turned off the small screen on her desk and ran her hand across her round belly. The baby was growing faster than she could ever anticipate. The swollen feet, painful breasts, night sickness, and fatigue were all worth it. In five months' time, she would have her own living and breathing version of Elias to love.

"Miss Wolfe." Her receptionist Sherry's voice sounded from the intercom in front of her. "There's a call for you on line one."

Ava pressed a button on the device. "Who is it?"

"His name is Mike Cordon from *The Coastal Times*."

Ava let out a groan. The man was a thorn in her side, constantly hounding for information about her baby's father. "Take a message, Sherry. I'm too busy to take calls."

"Okay." She clicked off and returned a few moments later. "I'm sorry, Ava. Mike's extremely persistent. He won't hang up until he talks to you. Do you want me to put him onto someone else?"

She sighed. "No, put him through." When her phone started ringing, she waited a few beats before answering. "Ava Wolfe speaking."

"Ava," Mike said, "I get the sneaking suspicion that you're avoiding my calls."

"How many times do I have to tell you to bugger off? I should be asking how you found out where I worked. I never disclosed my new employer."

Mike chuckled into the phone. "I'm a journalist, Ava. It's my job to investigate. Besides, I rely on my network of sources to siphon information to me."

"Did the same source try to sell you my park photographs?"

"No, I wasn't aware they existed until it was printed Sydney wide. It seems you have a leak in your pool."

"What do you want, Mike?" Ava demanded, growing increasingly frustrated. She had reports to write, numbers to crunch, and phone calls to make before six o'clock. She didn't have time to listen to his allegations.

"Who's the father of your baby?"

"I'm surprised your sources didn't tell you. You seem to know everything else."

"Okay, I'll be the first to admit they don't know everything. But you do. Why did Elias Dorne resign from Blue Tail after practically saving the company? I don't trust what I've read in the papers."

"They print the truth, Mike. It was Elias's decision to leave."

"Surely he told you why."

"No comment."

"Come on, Ava. We've been through a lot together. Give me something." When his plea was met with silence, he added. "Your resignation stunned the business world. Why did you quit so soon after Mr. Dorne?"

"Didn't you watch my press conference?" Ava asked. "I discussed my reasonings there. I will not talk about this further. Mr. Cordon, I have work to do. Please leave your questions with my secretary and I will send the answers to you shortly."

"Miss Wolfe, you're a hard woman to crack, but I'll get my answers one day," Mike said. "Good luck with your pregnancy."

When she heard the dull phone tone in her ear, Ava let out a breath of relief. She replaced the receiver back in its cradle and drained her glass of water sitting nearby. Her hands trembled. Mike's determination to find out the truth of her baby's father shook her more than she realised. She had turned her back on everyone to ensure Elias and their child would remain safe from public prejudice. One day she might reveal everything in a TV interview or magazine article, but right now, Ava had sacrificed her life for the ones she loved.

She packed up her purse and exited her office, striding passed Sherry on the way out. "I'm going to lunch. I'll be back in an hour."

The brunette smiled back. "I'll hold your calls, Ava."

"If it's urgent, I have my mobile." She took the lift down

to the ground floor and stepped into the warm afternoon. Merton was a little town two hours outside of Sydney. The township had a population of thirty thousand people and it was the perfect size for Ava to live undisturbed.

The streets were lined with cars waiting for parking spots and school kids dashing in and out of the local milk bar. In any other circumstance, Ava would've thought Merton was idyllic, but the rent was dirt cheap and people tended to keep to themselves.

Ava rounded the corner and ran straight into Daisy. The two women stared at each other, stunned, clutching their handbags to their chests. Ava felt like a diminutive mouse in Daisy's presence. The woman looked spectacular. Her wavy locks sashayed down her shoulders like spun gold and her enviable body was on display in skinny jeans and a peach top.

Her lush pink mouth forced a smile. "Ava, what a surprise to see you here."

"I was going to say the same thing. What are you doing in Merton?"

"My jeweller is out this way. He's the only one that does things how I like them." Daisy's gaze dropped to Ava's stomach and something dark crossed her features. "Well, you've definitely popped."

"Oh yes, I suppose I have."

"How much longer do you have now?"

"Twenty-two weeks give or take. The baby's growing very fast these days."

Daisy shifted her weight to another heel, a worried crease forming between her brows. "Do you know what you're having?"

"I find out in three weeks," Ava said proudly.

Daisy put her hand out tentatively towards Ava's belly. "Do you mind?"

"Go ahead." It felt strange having her former lover's

fiancée stroke her pregnant stomach. Daisy remained tight-lipped as she bent over, her head close to Ava's belly, waiting for the baby to move. "Has she kicked yet?"

"I get some fluttering but the baby won't do real acrobatics for another few weeks."

"It must feel weird to have something inside you moving around." Daisy extracted her hand and stood up. "Pregnancy freaks me out a bit."

"It's no different than having your man inside you. You get used to it."

Spots of colour reddened Daisy's cheeks and she cleared her throat. "I haven't seen you around Sydney for a while. Did you move to Merton?"

"I've been here for a month. Didn't you see my press conference regarding my resignation?"

When Daisy shook her head, Ava thought it was strange for her *not* to see it, since she was the catalyst for Ava's move out of the city.

"I've been busy planning my wedding. I don't watch the news." *There's the old Daisy.*

Trying hard to remain civil, Ava said, "Planning a wedding is an exciting time. How is everything going?"

"Don't you mean how Elias is doing?" The iciness in Daisy's voice cut Ava to the core. She knew it was a waste of time trying to be friendly to this girl. The bridge between them had long been burned.

"I was his friend and employer. I'm just asking an innocent question."

Her lips pouted. "He's fine. Back to his old ways of working so hard that I hardly see him. I'm beginning to think he doesn't want to be with me."

"He's a workaholic. It has nothing to do with you. Men like Elias are hard to tame out of their ways." She forced a smile of her own. "It was nice seeing you, Daisy. I better get back to work. Good luck for the future." Not waiting for a response, she turned and walked briskly back to the office, allowing tears of defeat to stream down her face.

~ ~ ~

Elias glanced around his boxed-filled unit and bit back a curse. Daisy's shit was everywhere, spilling onto his countertops, the dining room table, the couch, and even the bathroom. He used to take pride in his white-carpeted and white-walled bachelor pad before Hurricane Daisy blasted in. He couldn't walk into the kitchen without side-stepping clothes, shoes, and jackets lying all over the floor. His two-bedroom unit was too small to accommodate the extra stuff.

He heard Daisy humming in the bedroom, probably shoving her clothes into his walk-in wardrobe. Okay, so he agreed in letting her move in, but not so soon. His impending wedding was five months away and weighed heavily on his mind. Every time he thought of Ava or the baby, he was struck by bolts of guilt. How could he shut himself out when all he wanted to do was be a good father?

Daisy emerged from the bedroom, holding an empty box. She tossed it into the growing mound by the front door. "That's should do it. All my clothes have found a new home."

Elias grabbed a perspiring beer in the fridge and drained it. "That's wonderful, Daisy."

Sensing some hostility, she brushed past him to grab her own drink. "I saw Ava the other day," she said, her eyes studying him over the rim of the glass.

"What?" Elias jerked to a stop, his heart fluttering at the sound of her name. "When did you see her?"

"I bumped into her in Merton when I picked up my earrings. She's looking good, Elias. Her belly is getting bigger."

"Daisy, don't do this. Don't start a fight," Elias scolded. "I'm too tired to deal with your jealousy. Leave Ava alone."

He swung his arm around the unit. "You got what you always wanted. You got my life."

When Daisy slammed her glass down, Elias heard a crack, unsure if it was the glass or his granite countertop. "What do you see in her?" she asked through narrowed eyes. "Was it the red hair or her seniority? You know the reality is never like the fantasy. You would've seen her true colours eventually."

Elias brushed his hand through his hair and turned his back, not wanting to look at her. "I have no idea what you're talking about. I'm done discussing this, Daisy. We've had too many conversations about my ex-boss. Got it?" He walked towards the bedroom and heard Daisy marching after him down the hall.

"Don't you walk away from me!" she shrieked.

Elias spun around and caught her wrists so fast she recoiled in fear. "When did you become so cold?" He loosened his grip on her and Daisy jerked away, cowering in the corner of the room. "What happened to you, Daisy? You're not the same woman I grew up with. Fell in love with." He sighed. "Look, I understand it's been a testing time, but look where we are. We're going to get married. Surely that would make you feel whole."

A fire ignited behind her eyes and Daisy catapulted off the wall. "I lost a piece of my heart when you started fucking your boss!"

Elias's blood ran ice cold before regaining his composure. *Deny, deny, deny.* "You're yanking my chain, Daisy. Nothing happened between Ava and me."

"Stop lying to me!" She ran to an open box and violently rummaged through it, tossing things over her shoulder. She pulled out an envelope and spewed its contents onto the bed. Piles of photographs covered the mattress, capturing Elias's liaison with Ava at the shed and the park. He picked them up one by one as Daisy screamed at him.

"You broke me, Elias," she cried. "You were supposed to remain faithful to me. That was all I asked! You defied and humiliated me by sleeping with that whore! I can't imagine what you'll be like when we're married."

Elias deserved every word Daisy threw at him because she was right. He'd deceived their relationship by ripping it apart, using his body to pleasure another woman.

But, as he studied the photographs, radiating with a combination of sickness and rage, he realised Daisy was also to blame. Her deceit would indelibly mark the end of their relationship. Enraged, he gathered a handful of photos and ripped them into shards, throwing them across the mattress. "Why did you accept my proposal if you knew about Ava?"

Daisy sat down on the edge of the bed, twisting her diamond engagement ring around her finger. "Do you think I'm stupid, Elias? Your proposal was nothing more than a distraction to what was happening at the office. You broke my heart going behind my back like that! You shattered it into a million pieces."

"You had no right to follow me around like a stalker," Elias shot back, trying his hardest to restrain the anger rolling inside him. "You betrayed my trust, Daisy. You and I are more similar than I thought." He reached for her and she rebuffed him, shoving him away. "I had one indiscretion. Am I going to be punished for it for the rest of my life?"

"You mean the baby you put inside Ava?"

"What?" Elias glared at her, ignoring the cold chill sparking along his nape.

Her eyebrows cinched together. "I'm surprised you don't deny it since you've been denying everything else." She cocked her head to the side. "You wanna know how I found about your bastard child? I knew something was up for weeks leading up to the park. Ava's face was seen less on TV and you were acting so strange and distant. I'd thought you were hooking up again. But when I followed you to the park and saw you stroke her belly, I knew in my heart that my fears had come true. You're a cheater. Now, the whole country knows too!"

"I can't believe I'm listening to this. You can berate me all you want, Daisy, but you acted just as badly."

Daisy flew off the bed and shoved a trembling finger in Elias's face. "Me? How am I the bad one here? Did I put my dick in another woman and act like it was okay? I feel like I'm losing control of this, Elias, and it scares me."

Gritting his teeth, Elias crossed his arms over his chest. "I'm glad it frightens you because you don't deserve my love, Daisy. I'm suffocating when I'm around you." He marched to the wardrobe and yanked shirts and trousers off the hangers, tossing them onto the bed. Daisy watched on silently, her heated navy gaze glaring into him. The more clothes he buried into a bag, the more agitated she became. "Where are you going?"

"I'm out of here." He heaved his backpack onto his shoulder and walked to the door. "I need time to think about us. I can't be in the same room as you right now."

"You're going to her, aren't you?" Derision dripped from her lips.

Unresponsive, Elias tore the bedroom door open and sauntered through the apartment. He growled with frustration when he ran into one of Daisy's boxes, kicking it aside. He had no idea where he was going, but if he stayed another minute in this unit, he would do something he would regret.

Chapter 22

"Mum, do you want a cup of tea?" Ava asked, pulling a cup down from the cabinet. She could hear the TV blaring in the living room and pictured her mother glued to her soap operas. It had been wonderful having her mother back in her life, helping her prepare for the baby and building a foundation for her future. Things were going to change from now on. Her life as a high-profile publishing mogul was in the past.

"Mum, did you hear me?"

"Ava. Come here, honey." Veronica's voice sounded from the foyer, muted by the voices on the television.

"Mum?" Ava left the cup on the bench to investigate. She wandered through the living room and gasped when Elias stood in entryway with her mother. A backpack was slung over his shoulder and he wore a crumpled shirt. His eyes were heavy with fatigue.

"Elias, what are you doing here?"

A small smile lifted his lips. "I left Daisy."

Veronica cleared her throat and backed away. "I'll leave you to it. I'll be in the kitchen if you need anything."

When her mother was out of eyeshot, Ava ran up to Elias and pulled him into an embrace, wrapping her arms tightly around his neck. He smelled of sandalwood and male sweat. "Did you really do it?"

Burying his face into the nook of her neck, he replied, "She told me everything, Ava. She deceived me. Even after all these years, I feel like I don't know her at all." He pulled away to look at her, gently caressing her cheek with the pad of his thumb. "You were right all along. Daisy was bad for me."

Ava stepped away and escorted him into the living room. The television had been turned off. "How did you know where I lived?"

Elias sat down on the couch. "Daisy told me she'd seen you in Merton. I knew you wouldn't tell me where you were so I contacted Liam."

"He told you?"

He smirked. "I had to buy your location with a six pack of beer."

Ava rubbed her hands together. "Elias, you can't be here. Daisy will be wondering where you are. You can stay the night but you'll have to leave in the morning."

"I left her," he said, sliding across the cushion towards her. "It's over between Daisy and me. I want to be with you." He reached out and stroked her hand. A rush of ecstasy sparked inside Ava at his touch. "I've made my decision, Ava."

"No, you haven't. You made a commitment to Daisy and you have to stick to it. What can I offer you, Elias? A constant spotlight following you around everywhere? That's not living." The words hurt but they were needed. She wouldn't allow him to destroy his life.

"Why do you keep pushing me away?" Elias asked. "I thought you wanted to be with me."

Ava bit at her bottom lip. A huge part of her wanted to be with Elias forever. But the logical side of her knew it was impossible. There were too many things weighing against them. Daisy. The press. Her own conscience.

"Maybe in another lifetime, Elias, but not this one." She glimpsed at the clock on the wall in the kitchen and her stomach grumbled. It was time for another snack. All she did was eat now. "Mum made a delicious chocolate cake earlier. Do you want a slice?"

"When will you give me an answer?" Elias pressed as he followed her into the kitchen.

"It's never going to happen between us." She pulled the cake out of the fridge and cut two slices. She watched Elias in the corner of her eye as she handed him the plate. He looked defeated, with his slumped shoulders and downturned lips. Ava reasoned that he wasn't thinking straight. He was coming off the high from his fight with Daisy.

"When do you find out the gender?" Elias's voice sounded close behind her as they returned to the living room.

"I go to the doctors in a fortnight. The scan is between eighteen to twenty-two weeks."

"Would you mind if I came with you?"

"What would Daisy think?"

"I don't care. I want to be there when you find out."

"I guess you can come." Ava sliced into her cake with a fork, unsure why she was feeling uncomfortable. Wasn't this what she wanted? Being a family with Elias pushed her to keep going every day, but things changed the moment a diamond ring was put on Daisy's finger. It didn't matter how many times Elias left her. It didn't feel right being with him, especially if he turned up at her doorstep unannounced. It was still adultery in her eyes and she never wanted to be associated with that word again.

~ ~ ~

Veronica's dramatic soap operas didn't settle the unease in Elias's gut. He sat beside her on the couch, robotically stirring a teaspoon in his mug. His second helping of cake sat on the coffee table untouched.

Ava was upstairs taking a shower, leaving him to watch TV with her odd mother. He was a fool for coming here tonight. His misguided intentions had led him to a woman who obviously didn't want to see him. The perfect "O" shape of Ava's lips when she had entered the foyer imprinted on his memory. She was surprised to find him in her home, her safe place. As much as she wanted to end their coupling, he couldn't get her of his head. He would fight for her. No matter what.

"What are your intentions for my daughter?" Veronica's soft voice penetrated his thoughts.

Elias placed his cup on the table and cleared his throat. "Um . . . I'm not sure how much Ava has told you about us."

"I know enough, son. I know my unborn grandchild is your baby." Veronica twisted in her seat so she could face him. "Ava has always been secretive with her private life. Even to me. I didn't even know she was marrying Liam until a week after the wedding."

"Is that why you disliked him?"

Her eyebrow hooked. "I don't like being deceived. Especially by my own daughter. It's only ever been Ava and me." She narrowed her eyes. "What has Ava told you about me, anyway?"

"Not a lot. She rarely mentioned family when we worked together. She was all about business."

A crooked smile hooked Veronica's lips. "That's Ava. She likes to hold things close to her chest. No one has ever gotten close to her. Even Liam. I'm surprised how far she let you in. You must be special to her."

"I hope so."

"Look, my daughter doesn't have a good track record with men. In fact, the media loves judging her on her particular lifestyle. Ava's a beautiful woman. Even as a child, she had a certain appeal towards men. She knew how to play them, how to make them tick. When she turned thirteen, my stress levels almost killed me. I was so worried for her welfare. She was a wild girl and I couldn't control her. So I snuck birth control pills into her cereal each morning and prayed she would be okay."

"Ms. Wolfe, Ava turned out perfectly," Elias said. "She's an extremely successful business woman. Despite what the press says, Ava is unlike anyone else I've ever met. There aren't a lot of female media moguls in her position. She hasn't let her past define her."

"People judge her for what's printed in the tabloids. She's not a cold bitch, just misunderstood. She's a woman in a man's world. No one understands her like I do. Ava needs to understand that life is fleeting." Veronica withdrew a tissue from her nightgown and dabbled her eyes. "For years, she's been so driven by her work that she's missed out on living. All her friends have moved on and had babies of their own."

She glanced at Elias and squeezed his hand. "I want you to know that I don't think this baby's a burden. In fact, it's saved my daughter. I know you'll make Ava very happy. Welcome to the family, son."

Elias detected no ridicule or disdain in Veronica's voice so he assumed Ava hadn't mentioned Daisy or the upcoming wedding. Perhaps Ava was playing her own game of happy endings without the harsh reality. Elias wanted a future with her—or at least try for one—imagining playing with their son or daughter in the backyard with the dog. Ava had broken his ways, disrupted the rules he had lived by for years. After his fight with Daisy, he just drove, eager to get to his destination. He wanted one last chance with Ava, to prove the spark between them still existed. If he felt nothing, he would move on. His impeding wedding was getting closer by the day. So what did he really want? He was torn between two forces—the volcano and the tornado—both volatile and strong. Who would offer him the better future? Stringing both women along went against everything he stood for. He had to make his choice before it was too late.

Chapter 23

"Do you want to know the gender?" the female radiographer asked.

A breath hitched in Ava's throat as she studied the black and white screen. Her baby looked alien, curled up inside her like a Mimosa leaf. She had worked hard during the last two weeks to prepare for the birth. The nursery was freshly painted with new carpet, there were toys, and a mahogany crib was adorned with the finest bedding. Everything was neutral. All she needed was a splash of colour—blue or pink.

She shot her hand out and a warm one enveloped hers. She turned her head and smiled at Elias towering above her. As much as she loved having him around, she couldn't ignore the emptiness in her gut. This *fling* with Elias wasn't real. He hadn't canceled the wedding like he said he would. It was if Elias was clinging to the hope of returning to Daisy if they didn't work out. Ava hated the feeling his false promises instilled in her.

"Do you want to know?" he asked, squeezing her hand.

Ava nodded numbly, hoping her smile was believable to everyone in the room. "Of course."

The radiographer smiled. "You're having a healthy little girl."

Elias pressed a kiss to Ava's forehead. "Isn't that wonderful, Ava. A girl!"

"Are you sure the baby's okay?" Dazed by the rush of emotions inside her, Ava was didn't even notice Elias's show of affection. "I haven't felt her move lately."

The woman handed her a tissue to rub the gel off her stomach. "Your little girl has a solid heartbeat and her stats look good. Every baby develops differently. You have nothing to worry about, Ava."

She pulled her shirt down and accepted Elias's arm as he helped her off the bed. "That's good to hear. When will I see you next?"

"Doctor Mills would like to see you at twenty-eight weeks for another growth scan. If you have any concerns, please contact us. We rather you be paranoid than sit at home worrying. Okay?"

Ava nodded, thanked the radiographer, and walked into the waiting room. Veronica was sitting by the door, tapping her foot anxiously. When she saw Ava approach, she bounced off the chair as if she was on fire.

"What is it? What is it?" she cried.

Ava gave her insurance card to the receptionist. "A girl."

Veronica's screams of joy disrupted the entire waiting room so much that Elias had to drag her out of the medical centre. Ava joined them in the carpark. They were embracing, talking excitedly to each other. Despite what the future may hold, this was the time for new beginnings.

After a stop for a celebratory lunch, Ava drove Veronica and Elias back home. She froze at the sight of Liam's car parked across the street. She had to double check the plates to make sure it was really him.

"Is that Liam?" Veronica asked from the backseat.

Unresponsive, Ava pulled into the driveway and turned off the ignition. She sat in silence, watching Liam emerge from his car, dressed in jeans and a T-shirt. It was the first time she'd seen him without a suit. In her peripheral vision, Elias's shoulders tensed.

"What the fuck is he doing here?" he hissed.

They excited the car and headed for the porch.

"Ava!" Liam's voice carried across the road.

She ignored him as she unlocked the front door, swinging it open for Veronica and her shopping bags. A long shadow cast over her and she turned to find Elias standing between her and Liam.

"What are you doing here?" he demanded.

"I should be asking you the same question," Liam retorted. "What are you doing with my ex-wife?"

"I don't see how that's your business, Liam."

Ava blew out a frustrated breath and intercepted the two men, coming up between them. "Liam, what do you want?"

His dark eyes narrowed. "I'm here on behalf of Daisy. She asked me to come."

"Are you her hand servant now?" Elias interjected. "Why hasn't she bothered to make an effort to come here herself?"

"She didn't want to see you play house with Ava. You haven't returned any of her calls!"

"We're taking a break."

"Come on, Elias." Liam chuckled. "You're being delusional. The wedding isn't far away. You've said nothing about calling it off."

"Hey, cut it out!" Ava drummed her fists against the men's chests, drawing their attention. "I don't want any arguing." Her eyes narrowed on Liam. "Go home. You shouldn't be here. Daisy's a grown woman. She doesn't need a keeper."

"I'm not her Goddamn keeper, Ava. I'm just her friend. Daisy was too ashamed to confront the woman carrying her fiancé's baby. So she asked me to speak with you instead."

Ava rolled her eyes. "Come on, Liam. You expect me to believe that bullshit? What does she want?"

Liam jerked his chin towards Elias. "Him. She wants her man back. Give him up, Ava. You're not going to win this war."

"Elias doesn't belong to me. I know that. But he's is the only support system I have left, besides mum. He's here because I asked him to be."

Liam rested against the doorframe, one leg cocked. "Look, I don't know what kind of arrangement you've got here, but Daisy wants what is rightfully hers. You can't go around stealing men, Ava. You have a history of it, you know."

"I didn't steal him from anyone. Elias and I just happened organically." When she turned to him, she noticed Elias's posture was combative—back straight, arms crossed over his chest, lips drawn downwards. His navy eyes were narrowed and she was certain he was grinding his teeth. He was holding back.

Ava didn't know what she wanted anymore and it was becoming too hard to handle. Either she had Elias or she didn't. There was still a fragment of him that still belonged to Daisy.

She touched his arm gently, snapping him out of his reverie. "Maybe it's best you go," she said softly. "Go home to Daisy. She obviously misses you. I appreciate you being here for me today."

"I'm not going anywhere while he's hanging around," he shot back, jerking his chin at Liam. "I don't trust him."

"What don't you trust me with?" Liam said. "Is it Ava?" He wiggled a menacing finger at him. "You know, the baby should've been mine. Did she tell you that we tried conceiving for years? We went through IVF, counselling, and even started the adoption process. But you fucking knocked her up after a one-night stand!"

A growl escaped Elias's lips before he launched full speed at Liam. He threw all his weight into his opponent, slamming them against the wall. He heaved a punch into Liam's face and Ava heard a crack. Liam fought back, despite his broken nose, kicking and screaming so loud Veronica came out with a baseball bat.

"What's going on out here?" Her voice was barely audible over the men's grunts and curses.

"Mum, stay back," Ava warned. She jumped out of the way as the men tumbled to the floor, throwing punches and ripping each other's shirts. It pained her to see them fighting over her. But what could she offer them? She was used goods. Damaged. No one deserved her love. It would only destroy them.

"Stop!" she cried, pulling at Elias's shirt with all her strength. "You must stop. Get up, Liam. Get off, Elias!"

Elias pushed Liam onto his back and straddled him, legs on either side of his hips. Elias's bloodstained lips were pulled into a vicious sneer, a leer that spooked Ava. She never intended for him to be pulled in so deep. If she could take everything back, she would.

She stepped behind the grunting and cursing men and squeezed her eyes shut, clenching her fists. "STOP IT NOW! I'M NOT WORTH IT!"

Her cries fell on deaf ears, except for her mother's, who she heard screaming out her name, her fingers pulling at her cardigan frantically. Growling in frustration, Liam propelled Elias back with so much force that he toppled into Ava, knocking her to the floor.

Veronica's screams froze the men in mid-fight. They stopped, glanced around, and gasped in unison at Ava on the ground cradling her belly.

"What have you boys done?" Veronica pushed the men out of the way and kneeled beside Ava, stroking her forehead lovingly. "Are you all right?"

"I'm fine."

Veronica set her stare on Liam and screamed, "Call an ambulance!"

Ava didn't know what happened after that. Her entire world was sucked into a soundless vacuum as she was taken to hospital. During the trip, she prayed for the baby to be okay. It hadn't been a hard fall and she was certain Veronica was over-reacting, but she was glad she'd inflicted some guilt on Liam and Elias. They had instilled so much pain on her already.

~ ~ ~

Ava awoke from a restless sleep. Rays of fractured sunlight bathed the small hospital room adorned with "Get Well" cards and flowers. Her mother lay slumped in a chair by the bed, a soft snore escaping her lips. Her hair was pulled back into an unwashed bun and the crumby remains of her lunch had gathered in her lap. Ava was comforted by her presence, forever grateful that Veronica had faithfully remained by her side, sharing tears of relief when the doctor reassured that the baby was uninjured from the fall.

A man shouted outside in the hall and her bedroom door burst opened. Liam entered the room and slammed the door behind him, momentarily blinded by flashing lights and camera crews.

"They're still out there?" Ava asked, accepting the bottle of water and sandwich he handed her.

Liam sat down in the chair next to Veronica. "The vultures never left. Channel Four and Nine are still in the halls and I told a reporter from Ten to fuck off. At least they'll have some content for the news tonight."

Ava unwrapped her sandwich. "I don't make headlines anymore. Why are they still interested in me?"

"You're a beautiful woman caught in the spotlight," Veronica replied, wiping sleep from her eyes. Liam handed her a cup of water and she drained it. "Your baby has only piqued their interest. You haven't publicly revealed the father so they're hungry for a story. I'm afraid it'll only get worse as your pregnancy continues." She patted Ava's knee. "But you're not alone, honey. I'm here for you."

Ava stared at her ham sandwich, listening to doctors and nurses berate the journalists in the hall. She was foolish to think she was free from public interest. It would never end until the press found another story more scandalous.

"Where's Elias?" she asked, reaching for her phone on the bedside table. There were no new texts.

Liam cleared his throat. "Elias's gone back to Daisy."

"Why did he go?"

"I told him too," Liam said without an iota of repentance. "He's not family."

Ava tossed her phone onto the bed in frustration. "And you're family? We are divorced, Liam. You don't get to make decisions for me anymore."

"Having your former employee at the hospital was making the journos curious. When I went for a piss, they asked me why Elias was here. It looked strange to them."

"What did you tell them?" Veronica probed. "My grandchild is in the middle of this disaster."

"I lied. I told them Elias was visiting a sick friend. They were so hungry for gossip that they swallowed it up."

Ava couldn't deny that Elias's absence created a massive void inside her. It swallowed her up like a black hole. She felt empty inside, soulless. Her dependence on him was frightening, yet the fight forced her to see the light. She couldn't do this anymore, couldn't be the third wheel in a relationship that only had one ending. She wanted answers. Needed closure. The love triangle had been going on long enough. The baby deserved a clean slate. She did too.

"Liam, please call security," she said, pulling the blankets up to her chin. "I wish to get some sleep before I'm discharged. I don't want the vultures following us home."

Chapter 24

Elias stood in the shadows of the hallway and listened to Daisy's sobs coming from the bedroom. Her crocodile tears were loud and intentional, a ruse to trap him into an apology for breaking her heart when he returned from the hospital. She knew where he'd been, and with whom, pleading with him to break the chains shackling Ava, Daisy, and him together.

For the first time in months, he felt ready to disconnect. His short fuse had almost caused the death of his unborn child. He'd stopped breathing when he saw Ava on the ground, clutching her stomach. He wasn't going to fight Liam anymore because he wasn't going to win. It was safer for Ava if he stepped away.

He entered the bedroom to find Daisy curled up on the bed, surrounded by a ring of crumpled tissues. Her engagement ring sat on the bedside table, winking in a beam of sunlight. There were times he felt like a rubber band, snapping back to her when things got rough, unable to sever the tie. He justified his affair with Ava as a moment of weakness, a union of two broken and lonely people.

But Ava was right when she said there was no future together. As a typical, hot-blooded male, Elias had listened to his dick instead of his heart and almost lost the most important person in his life—Daisy.

"Why aren't you happy?" he asked, resting a hip on the edge of the mattress. He picked up the diamond ring and circled it around his finger. "I'm home for good now. I'm never leaving you again."

"I don't believe that," Daisy spat, turning around, narrowing her red-rimmed eyes. "I feel like I'm locked in a constant battle with *her*. Who's going to win the coveted prize of Elias's love? I respected your wishes for a break because I love you. But I'm giving you one last chance, Elias. Make your choice. It's her or me."

"I choose you, Daisy." He slipped the ring back onto her finger, feeling the warmth of her skin on his palm. "It's always been you and me ever since we were kids. Let's get married. We can leave the meddling press and public interest behind us."

She raised a skeptical eyebrow. "How can I trust you won't stray again? You committed the ultimate betrayal by cheating on me. You created a child with another woman. I can't simply move on from this. Ava has collateral over you now. She's tied you down for the next eighteen years and she'll use the baby against you. I'm certain of it. How can I be your wife when there's another woman hanging over our heads?"

"Daisy, you'll have to learn to live with her being in our lives," he replied sternly. "I'm going to be a father to this child whether you like it or not."

"Do you still love her?"

Elias stood up with a groan and stared out the window. The streets were thick with traffic, congested, just like his thoughts. Love was a funny word. He never used it lightly, or sometimes not at all, when it came to describing his feelings for the people in his life. He loved his parents and Daisy, but when it came to Ava, he couldn't think of the right word to define how he felt about her. Their relationship was built on a crumbling foundation of lust and desire. Nothing more. There was a time when he thought he loved her, but it was only a mask, a form of escapism from his boring life. The excitement, danger, and passion he felt during their liaison was short-lived, but Ava's unusual teachings had created a businessman with drive and ambition. Elias knew what he wanted in life and Daisy was at the top of the list. "Let's talk about our future. We still have a wedding to plan."

She joined him by the window, wrapping her arm around his middle. "There's something else I need to tell you."

"What is it?"

"Do you remember the night you appeared on my parents' doorstep? We were on our break and you were drunk as a sailor?"

Elias dipped his head in shame. "How could I forget? I think your father almost shot me when I pushed him out of the way to get your bedroom."

"Could you blame him? Our wedding—which my parents paid for—was on the verge of being called off. You were the last person they wanted to see." She drew invisible circles on the window pane. "But I remember our lovemaking that night was so crazy hot." Daisy opened the bedside drawer and pulled something out. "I was going to tell you earlier but I wanted to choose the right time." She dropped a pregnancy test into his open hand.

Elias barely heard Daisy's soft voice in his ear. His heart beat like a drum as he turned the positive white stick over in his hands. Somewhere in the back of his mind, he must've known this would happen. He didn't remember much of the night he slept with Daisy, but he knew the sex was clumsy, drunken, and without reason. They didn't use protection. But why should it matter? They were getting married. It wasn't as if they were forbidden lovers caught in a tryst . . .

When he heard a sharp intake of breath, Elias snapped from his reverie and brought Daisy into an embrace. "I'm very happy, baby. How far along are you?"

She hesitated, biting her bottom lip. "Um . . . I don't have a scan or anything, but the doctor said I'm three weeks. It's still early days."

He kissed the top of her scalp, pushing the haunting image of Ava's face from his mind. Why did she appear at the thought of Daisy's baby? It wasn't like he was cheating on her. They were over. Done. He had so much to look forward to in his future. "A wedding and a baby all in the same year. We're going to have an interesting twelve months. We can celebrate the baby with your parents at lunch tomorrow. Do they know yet?"

She nodded. "I'm sorry, I told my mum first. I hope that's okay. There are some moments in life when a woman must confide in her mother."

"I understand. At least I won't ruin the surprise."

"Speaking of that, I have one request." Daisy cleared her throat and tossed a lock of blonde hair over her shoulder. "Please don't mention Ava or her baby over lunch, okay? I don't want anything to ruin our day. My parents are so excited for their first grandchild. They don't need a reminder of your indiscretion."

Elias blew sharply from his nose, unable to ignore the pang of hurt Daisy's words inflicted. "I'd never broadcast what happened with Ava if that's what you mean. I don't want to repeat myself, Daisy. It's over between her and me. Her name won't be mentioned over lunch."

A strange, sly smile crossed Daisy's face and she planted a big kiss on his lips. "Good." She turned on her heels and sauntered for the door. "What are you wanting for dinner? I have a craving for Thai food."

~ ~ ~

"Remember, Daisy, you're pregnant so stay clear from the cheese and wine," Olivia Henderson instructed as she handed her daughter the café menu.

"I know, Mum. But I love cheese and wine." A look of irritation crossed Daisy's face and she drained her soft drink, her sky-blue gaze locked on Elias. He saw it as a silent plea for back up. Lunch with Olivia and Donald Henderson was like eating with two bloodthirsty jackals. There was no chance of survival. Since his affair became public knowledge, Elias expected to fight for his place in the Henderson family. Their loyalty to him had waned. They saw him as a cheater, not good enough for their only child. But he was. He just hoped the baby would soften their hard exteriors.

"There are dishes on the menu you can have," he said, leaning over to point out the chicken breast and barramundi. "I'm looking at the T-bone myself. You don't have to restrict your diet completely. Just be weary of what you eat."

"Your fiancé is right, honey," Olivia mused. "I missed eating cheese and deli meats when I was pregnant with you. But you're a mother now. You make sacrifices for your children."

"Don't let your mother scare you." Donald's gruff voice cut across the table, attracting everyone's attention. "Just enjoy the experience."

A waiter materialised by the table and took their orders. As Elias watched the waiter disappear into the kitchen, he noticed a few curious glances thrown his way by other patrons. It didn't surprise him that he would have interest dining with Daisy and her parents. His face had been plastered across Australian newspapers, frolicking with another woman. Of course people were curious.

His gaze flickered upwards to Donald who glared back with a stern expression. He must've seen the curiosity as well. More lines of disapproval had etched into the man's forehead. It would take more than a grandbaby to heal this wound.

"Have you found your suit, Donald?" Elias asked, wishing the glass of water the waiter put in front of him was alcoholic.

Donald grunted. "Yes, it's just a simple black and white suit. Nothing fancy, son."

"I told Dad that he must incorporate our colour theme," Daisy interjected proudly. "His tie will match yours. Teal, I think. His boutonnière will be a simple red rose."

Olivia clapped her hands together. "It's going to be such a beautiful wedding. When's your final dress fitting, honey? They'll have to accommodate for your new bump."

"The dressmaker told me it's harder to let out a gown, but she said we still have time to make adjustments. I see her next week for another fitting." She reached over and squeezed Elias's hand. "I hope you won't mind me looking like a whale on our wedding day."

Elias subtly avoided the kiss Daisy aimed for his lips. He was unsure why he felt awkward discussing the baby in front of her parents. Maybe it was the guilt still bottled inside him, or perhaps it was Ava's face that haunted him. He swallowed the lump in his throat and said, "I don't care what you look like. I'll love you no matter what."

While Olivia cooed with sheer delight, Donald was harder to impress, grunting into his soda. Their food arrived on time and everyone silently dug into their fish and chips, salads, and T-bone steaks. The mood was lightened when the waiter delivered a bottle of wine to the table.

Elias practically dived for it, eagerly opening the bottle and pouring three wineglasses. He drained the liquid in half a second. He was about to get another glass when Olivia asked the table to put down their knives and forks.

"This won't take long," she promised, looking at Daisy with a tear in her eye. "Your father and I would like to give your wedding gift early." She lifted an envelope from her purse and placed it on the table. "We understand that planning a wedding and an upcoming arrival is expensive. It doesn't help to build a new life together when you have so much debt. Your father and I would like to help in some way." She handed the envelope to Daisy. "I hope this will help you find your dream home."

Daisy ripped the envelope open and let out a deafening scream. "Oh, Mum! You shouldn't have. We can't accept this."

Elias took the gift from her fingers and gasped at the amount written on the cheque. It was for thirty thousand dollars. "Olivia and Donald, you're very generous. But Daisy is right. We cannot accept this. That's a huge amount of money."

Olivia fluttered her hand in the air. "Elias, please. We've been saving up for this moment since Daisy was a little girl. She's our only child so we wanted to spoil her when she got married. Besides, you can't live in your little two-bedroom unit with a baby. You'll have no room."

"We'll have to sell it," Daisy interjected. "We can use the money to find a nice place outside of the city. I was thinking of the North Shore."

Elias slipped the cheque back into the envelope, an unease settling in his gut. His entire future had already been set out for him. Everything was happening so fast. Buying a house and having a family was further down his priority list. Still, he preferred to be on Donald's good side. He shot out his hand towards him. "It's incredibly generous of you and Olivia to offer the money. It'll definitely help us put down a house deposit."

They shook hands.

"It's my pleasure, Elias. My daughter is very important to me. As her parents, we only want the best for her, including who she spends the rest of her life with."

Elias took advantage of the silence around the table to order another beer. He didn't bother to ask if anyone else wanted anything.

Olivia reached across the table and squeezed her daughter's hand. "There's a new shoe shop that's opened across the road. Do you want to check out their collection? You'll need something to wear on your honeymoon."

"I have old ballet flats at the moment. I can always do with more shoes." Daisy turned to Elias. "I'm sure you and Dad can keep yourself occupied for twenty minutes. I won't be long." She planted a kiss on his cheek and took off with her mother across the road.

Elias smiled weakly at Donald. "Can I offer you another beer?"

The older man shook his head. "No. In fact, I'm glad the women have left. I want to speak with you privately."

Panic levels spiked inside Elias. "Oh, about what?"

"It's about the cheque we gave you," he said. "I want you to understand something: Olivia and I gifted you and Daisy the money in good faith that you will make my daughter happy. It's very important to me that you do."

"Of course, sir. I love your daughter. I always have her best interests at heart."

"Really? Look, I try to ignore the drivel that's printed in the papers these days. But I couldn't ignore the gossip written about you." He put his hands up. "I'm not going to ask you if the rumours are true about that other sheila, but Daisy is a passionate, young woman who loves you unconditionally. If she has forgiven you, then her mother and I have too." His steely gaze returned, piercing Elias to the core. "However, if I hear you've broken her heart again, I will put you down. You got that, son?"

Elias nodded numbly, trying his hardest to wipe the stricken expression off his face. "Yes, sir," he replied at last, struggling for a mental toehold. "You have my word. I will never hurt Daisy again."

"Good boy."

Chapter 25

Months Later

Elias averted his eyes from the computer screen and rubbed them with the heel of his palm. Outside, the vast cloudless sky was changing from pink to magenta, the sun dipping behind the city skyline. The office was empty and quiet as the last group of employees scattered to enjoy Friday evening. Elias was invited to join them for a beer, but he wasn't in the mood. He still had a pile of articles to write and advertisers to chase for money. In truth, he wasn't ready to go home.

He pressed the home button on his phone and an image of Daisy and her pregnant bump lit up the dim office. It took him some time to adjust to Daisy's pregnancy. Her weird food cravings, mood swings, and weight gain materialised all at once, smashing into him like a tidal wave. Work was the only respite he had from the craziness at home. The wedding was fourteen days away, adding more pressure to his overburdened shoulders. There was so much he could take before his resolve snapped. He tried his best to console Daisy during her hormonal tantrums when she blamed the pregnancy for her vile tempers. He'd accepted this as his life now, but he couldn't ignore the inner discomfort, an emptiness that nibbled at his conscience. He carried it around day and night, unable to determine what was making him feel ill. In the end, he reasoned it was the secret texts with Ava that contributed to his jitters. They had swapped text messages over the last few months, keeping each other updated on their lives. Elias wasn't prepared to rid her from his life just because Daisy told him to. They shared a connection that ran deeper than the child inside her.

His phone buzzed when a text came through. It was from Daisy.

Daisy: When will you be home? It's seven o'clock
Elias: I'm leaving now
Daisy: Can you please pick up the cake for the baby shower tomorrow? I won't have time
Elias: Yes, Daisy.
Daisy: Thanks. Kisses

Elias pocketed his mobile, turned off his computer and left the office. He walked through his unit door half an hour later cradling a cakebox in one arm and folders and paperwork in the other. The unit was infused with the aroma of stir fry, making his stomach grumble. He heard Daisy singing a pop song in the kitchen. He took a moment to savour this moment as he kicked off his shoes, knowing it would be short-lived. This was the Daisy he grew up with, loved, the Daisy he wanted to settle down with. He would be the first to admit that his affair with Ava had ultimately stripped away Daisy's innocence and placidity. She wasn't the same woman anymore.

He entered the kitchen and came up behind her at the stove, wrapping his arms around her swollen middle. She flinched at his touch and backed away, almost dropping the ladle in her hands.

"Elias, you startled me."

"I thought you heard me coming home," he argued, bending into the fridge to retrieve a beer. "You never let me touch you anymore."

Daisy rubbed her hands down her apron and welcomed him with a peck on his cheek. "I don't intentionally reject your affection, Elias. Sometimes I don't like to be touched. I just feel weird with this pregnancy. Do you know what I mean?"

"I do, but we haven't been intimate in two months. How do you think that makes me feel?"

She turned her back on him, returning to the stir fry. "I don't want to fight."

"We're not fighting." Elias spun her back around, planting two hands on her shoulders. "We're having a discussion. If you and I going to be married and raise a family together, we need to communicate. The baby isn't the only reason why you haven't let me touch you."

She blew out a breath and wandered into the living room. Elias followed her, perching on the edge of the couch, waiting for what she had to say.

"I'm happy the media interest surrounding you has died down," she said. "I don't think I could've dealt with the nagging paparazzi or flashing cameras. Particularly since I'm in a delicate position."

"I'm yesterday's news now, so I doubt you'll see my face in the paper again."

Her fair skin turned a shade darker. "I suspect you will when Ava gives birth. Her pregnancy made national headlines. I gather the birth will too. She's about due now, isn't she?"

"Yes, due the same week as our wedding."

"Oh, how unfortunate you'll be too busy getting married to attend the birth."

Gotcha. Daisy never hid her insecurities well, imprinted on her like a tattoo. "I wasn't going to anyway." Elias leaned towards her. "Is this why you're angry at me? Do you think I'm going to leave our wedding day to be with Ava?"

"A girl can only assume, can't she? Look at your history, Elias. I was always second best in the battle with Ava. My father is half expecting you to run out the door before I even walk down the aisle."

"Not going to happen."

"You promise?"

"I'm marrying *you*, aren't I? Daisy, you must move past this. Ava and I were a fling—a regrettable fling—and my guilt for hurting you still cuts deep. I'm with you. No one else."

She smiled. "I know you are but see it from my perspective. You're unpredictable, babe. I never know what's going through that head of yours."

Feeling as though they were spiralling into darker territory, Elias changed the subject by picking up the RSVPs to Daisy's baby shower. "How many women are you expecting to attend the shower?"

"About thirty or so. I don't want a large group. I've invited people whom I can trust because I don't want this event leaking to the press. I don't want more unwanted attention."

"Do you need me to do anything?"

"No, Mum and I have everything sorted out. She'll run the last few errands I have so I can attend my next scan mid-week."

Elias's eyebrows snapped together. "Hang on. Shouldn't I be attending the appointment with you?"

"I booked it on Wednesday because it was the only time they had left. It didn't occur to me that you might be at work."

"What time is it? I can take the hour off," Elias insisted. "I would like to go and see our baby."

An odd expression overcame Daisy's face and she shook her head, dismissing his suggestion. "I want to go by myself, if that's okay. I'll bring home the scan picture if they give me one."

Elias was welcomed by the familiar jitters in his gut. "I'm the father, Daisy. I deserve to go. Why won't you let me?"

"I don't know," she mumbled, playing with a loose thread on her cardigan. "I can't put a reason to it. It's just something I want to do on my own. There'll be lots more scans to go to. Okay?"

"Is it because it won't be the first time I've attended a scan?" Elias probed. "Does this have to do with Ava?"

Daisy shook her head, causing her loose curls to bounce. "Stop making accusations. Your affair has damaged me, Elias. It's something I cannot brush underneath the rug. I need time to heal. Of course I'm bitter about the fact you've already been to a scan to see your bastard child." Daisy shot her hand up when he tried to object. "The scan on Wednesday should've been your first time." She stood up and gazed down at him, her eyes watery with tears. "Elias, you must accept that I will forgive you in time. But how can I when you'll have a child with another woman?" She turned and headed towards the bedroom. "Dinner is ready on the stove. I'm not hungry tonight, so please dish out yourself."

~ ~ ~

On the morning of the baby shower, Elias drove out of the city to visit his mother. He couldn't bear being around Daisy after their argument. The more she belittled his past actions, the more he drifted away from her in mind and body, detaching himself from his responsibilities. He needed familiarity and support from someone other than Daisy's closest circle. He didn't have friends nearby so he reasoned a coffee with his mother was long overdue.

He parked the car outside a rustic, vegan café and walked in to find Karen nose deep in a newspaper. He squinted his eyes to determine if his face was on the front page or not. She glanced up, saw him standing opposite her and tossed the paper aside. "Oh, my beautiful boy. You're here." Karen pulled him into a lung crushing hug. "Look at you. You're still so handsome."

"Hi, Mum."

"Can I get you something? A soy chai latte perhaps?"

He nodded as the waiter approached their table. "Sounds good." He gave his order and pulled out a chair, observing the potted cacti adorning the table. "I didn't know you were vegan, Mum."

"I'm not," she said, "but I've heard fabulous things about this place." She thumbed over her shoulder. "Did you see the dairy- and egg-free cheesecake out the front? It's to die for, apparently."

"We can share a slice."

Karen picked up the table water and poured two glasses. "So how's the wedding jitters going? You're a week away from being a Mr. and a Mrs."

Elias bit at his bottom lip. He'd always respected his relationship with his mother. He could tell her anything. "I'm having second thoughts about it, actually."

"What? How come?"

He lifted a shoulder. "I can't define it, Mum. Daisy isn't the same woman I fell in love with. She's bitter and hardened. She doesn't even want me to go to the scan with her next week. I'm living with a stranger."

"Honey, she's been through a trauma. While I don't condone what you did with that other woman, you have to see from Daisy's perspective. She's probably anxious and concerned about the future. There aren't a lot of women out there who would take back a cheating partner. I must give her credit for it. She must really love you."

"At first I thought her attitude was due to the pregnancy hormones. But I don't think it is. It runs deeper than that." He swallowed the lump in his throat. "Mum, do you know that Ava is pregnant too?"

"Of course I do. It was hard to ignore her face splashed across every newspaper and trash magazine. I understand that you were close to her. Did she ever disclose who fathered her baby? It's a big mystery." A spark of mischief lit up her eyes. "Was it her ex-husband, Liam?"

Elias inhaled slowly, letting his lungs fill up with air. He couldn't predict how his mum would react about her first grandchild born out of wedlock. She was his last support beam. Without her, everything would crumble on top of him. "Mum, I'm the father of Ava's baby. She never disclosed my name to the press. She destroyed her reputation in order to save mine."

Karen's cheeks drained of colour and she brushed her hand across her face. "Oh, right. How long have you been sleeping with this woman?"

"It was a one-night stand. It was a mistake."

"You're damn right, Elias. I didn't think you were the serial monogamist type."

Elias let out a long-winded sigh. "How many times do I have to spell it out? I never intended to cheat on Daisy. I had a moment of weakness. Now, I'm being punished for it by you and her." He inhaled sharply. "In all honesty, I never thought Ava would get pregnant."

"I didn't raise you to be ignorant, son. Women can fall pregnant at any time. You had no right to cheat on Daisy. She's been good to you." Karen's face was creased into lines of motherly disapproval. Elias had never seen her look so disappointed before. After a beat, she added, "Was Ava on the pill?"

"Yes," Elias replied.

"Does Daisy know about the baby?"

"Yes, she does. I don't know what to do. At the moment, I see no way out."

Karen reached across the table and squeezed his hands. "There's always a way out if you truly want it. You must make a decision and you must make it very soon. If you're having doubts about this wedding, then you should listen to your gut. It never lies." She sighed. "Elias, I wished you had come to me earlier. We could've worked out what to do. When is Ava due?"

"Same week as the wedding."

"Have you spoken to her recently?"

"We speak once a week. I have to be vigilant so Daisy doesn't catch me. Last time she called, she told me the baby's in position so her doctor thinks she'll go any time. I don't want to miss the birth, Mum."

Pity filled Karen's eyes with tears and she cupped his face in her hands. "Listen to your heart, Elias. Once you've signed the dotted line, you'll be committed to Daisy and her child. Besides, how can you be sure Ava wants to be with you? The last thing I want you to do is make the wrong mistake and miss out on a good future."

"Mum, I'm being punished for my mistake every day. I feel like I'm being torn down the middle by both women. I don't want to disappoint either of them. I can't leave Daisy at the altar wondering what happened."

"Honey, I wish I had the answers for you. This is a decision you must make on your own. If you believe you'll have a bright and happy future with Daisy, then I suggest you bury your past with Ava and move on. You have so much to lose if you don't."

His mother didn't give the answer he was hoping for, but Elias knew she was right. When Daisy returned home on Wednesday with the scan of their child, it would make everything real, determined. They would be a family. In the back recess of his mind, shadows of doubt started to grow and he prayed he was making the right choice.

Chapter 26

Ava needed a crane to get out of her chair. The massive boulder around her middle was making it hard to do simple, daily tasks. Every morning was a battle to roll out of bed and get to work without knocking her baby bump into things. She was lucky to have empathetic co-workers who helped with lifting and running errands she couldn't do. Even her secretary had gotten into the habit of leaving a peppermint tea on her desk before she waddled in of a morning. But Ava hated feeling vulnerable, having people run personal errands for her. She never instilled the practice as a CEO, and reminded her staff that things would change when she came back from leave. If she did at all . . .

Her pregnancy had altered her thinking, changed her inner wiring. She wanted the best upbringing for her child, to grow up in a safe and loving environment. She never planned to be a single parent but accepted her fate. As much as it hurt not to have Elias by her side, it was placating to hear his voice on the end of her phone every week.

A knock sounded at her door and Ava's secretary Sherry poked her head in. "Can I get you anything, Miss Wolfe? A tea or a Danish perhaps?"

Ava glimpsed from her computer. "No, it's fine. Alfred has delivered my sandwich already."

The brunette smiled and tentatively entered her office. "Please forgive my intrusiveness, but you must be pretty excited about the birth. How much longer do you have?"

"I'm thirty-eight weeks now, so my doctor said I can go

at any time. And yes, I'm very excited. Terrified at the same time too."

"I'm a mum of three boys," Sherry explained. "It's normal to be scared, Miss Wolfe. But after all the pain and pushing, you'll have a beautiful new baby to hold in your arms. That outweighs everything else. Will your mother be with you?"

"Of course. Veronica is my sole support system. She's been with me to every scan and doctor's appointment. I wouldn't have ever done it without her."

"Mothers are wonderful like that." Sherry retreated for the door, wrapping her fingers around the knob. "If you need anything else, please buzz me, Miss Wolfe."

"Thank you, Sherry." Ava waited until the secretary had closed the door before returning to her work. She was half way through writing a report when the baby kicked abruptly, startling her. She leaned back in her chair and rubbed her hand across her belly, watching the skin expand as her daughter attempted somersaults inside her.

"You're active today, little one," Ava cooed. Feeling parched, she pushed her chair back and wandered across the office to her mini bar. As she leaned down to open the door, an immense build-up of pressure almost winded her, causing Ava to collapse onto the cabinet lining the wall.

"Oh!"

She exhaled through narrowed lips, resting her forehead on her arm, allowing another wave of Braxton Hicks to pass. This one was more intense than the prodromal labour contractions she experienced during the week. Keeping her breathing shallowed, Ava straightened slowly, stabilising herself against the cabinet.

A warm liquid rushed down her inner thigh, creating a pool between her feet. "Oh shit. No! Not now." Panic interlaced with fear as Ava remained rooted to the spot, unsure whether to move to get her phone. Instead, she screamed. "Sherry!"

Her office door swung open and Sherry bolted inside. Upon seeing Ava bent over the cabinet, moaning in pain, she cursed under her breath and ran to the phone on Ava's desk. "Don't worry, Miss Wolfe. We'll get you to the hospital in time. Hold on for me, honey."

Ava responded with a panicked scream, uncaring if half the office heard her. "Get me an ambulance now!"

~ ~ ~

Most people would be excited on their wedding day. Not Elias. All he could think about was Ava and their baby. He picked up his suit jacket from the bed and slipped it on, studying his reflection in the mirror. He was a man divided between two halves of his heart. One was captained by loyalty and the other, passion. His heart would never be whole until he chose the right woman.

He fingered the silky soft petals of the rose pinned to his lapel. There were days he felt just as delicate, easy to bruise and tear. So why did he think marrying Daisy was the worst decision to make? A part of him didn't want to break her heart, but she hurt him too, selling her photographs to the press. They were both tainted and damaged souls.

His mobile phone buzzed, and he crossed the room to answer it. It was Ava's number. He answered it without hesitation. "Ava, are you okay?"

"It's Veronica, Ava's mother."

"Is Ava all right?"

Veronica's voice was partially muffled by a woman moaning in the background. "Ava's in labour right now. She's ten centimetres dilated and ready to push. If you want to be here for the birth, I highly suggest you get your ass over here right now."

Elias's shoulders slumped with defeat and he collapsed onto the bed. "Veronica, I can't. It's my wedding day. I'm about to walk into the church."

"I don't know what to say, honey. The baby could arrive at any time. You're more than welcome to visit after your daughter is born." Her end went silent for a moment and Elias gripped the phone so hard his fingers ached. "Elias, I have to go," Veronica said at last. "Call me back on this number when you can."

Elias remained seated on the bed, his spine razor straight, his phone still attached to his ear. Ava needed him. Their daughter needed him. This was the sign he'd been praying for. He glanced at his watch. The ceremony was starting in fifteen minutes. He didn't have time to sneak away for the birth and come back. The decision he made now would change his life forever.

Someone knocked on his bedroom door and Karen poked her head in. "Honey, are you ready? I got a call from Olivia. They're ten minutes away. It's time to head to the church." When he remained speechless, Karen entered the room, concern splashed across her face. "Elias, what's wrong?"

"Ava's in labour right now."

"Oh, what do you want to do?" She sat down next to him.

The pressure of tears built behind his eyes and he curled his fingernails into his palms to divert the pain. "I don't know, Mum. I've never been so unsure of anything in my life." He rested his head on her shoulder, craving her reassurance and empathy. "I love Ava. I should be there with her for the birth of our baby."

"Honey, if you are certain of your feelings, you must listen to your heart."

"What about Daisy?"

Karen took his face in her hands and stared deep into his eyes. "Do you really want to go through with this wedding?"

Without an iota of repentance, Elias replied, "No."

Karen dropped her hands into her lap. "There's your answer." She patted his thigh. "You better tell Daisy before you leave. Allow her some dignity. This is the biggest day of her life. She doesn't need to be humiliated in front of everyone."

Elias kissed his mother's cheek and bounded out of the room. He ran down the hallway searching for Daisy. Knowing his fiancée, she would stop for a touch up before walking down the aisle. He caught a wisp of a white gown entering a room down the hallway and he dashed towards it.

He barged into the room before the door closed, startling Daisy and her three bridesmaids.

"Elias, what are you doing here?" Daisy shrieked, leaping out of sight. "You can't see me before the wedding."

"I need to speak with you urgently."

A flicker of fear flashed across her face before she waved her hand in the air. "Fine. It's okay, girls. I'll meet you at the church."

Her bridesmaids begrudgingly left the room. Elias waited until the door shut behind them before pulling Daisy out of her hiding spot. She looked like a princess in her white strapless wedding gown. Her golden hair fell in soft waves around her shoulders. Her makeup was effortless and clean. Her beauty stung him.

"What's wrong with you?" she asked, crossing her arms over her chest. "Do you have cold feet?"

He dropped his gaze to the carpet, unable to look her in the eye. "I can't do this."

Daisy's eyebrows snapped together. "Excuse me. You can't do what?"

He motioned the air between them. "Us. I can't marry you."

Daisy's face crumpled in distress, her perfectly painted lips pulled downwards. "It's Ava, isn't it?"

Elias swallowed hard. "I'm sorry, Daisy. I really am."

Fresh tears streamed down her face, creating white streaks on her cheeks. "Is that all you can say to me? We have history, Elias. What do you have with this woman? Nothing!" She rubbed her hand across her eyes, ruining her makeup. "Even on my wedding day, this fucking woman has power over you. Why did you decide today is the day to break up with me?"

"Ava's in labour," Elias said carefully. "She's having my baby, Daisy. I need to be there for her."

"So you're choosing her over me again. Why am I not surprised? We are getting married today! Can't you see that? You inexplicably promised *me* a future when you proposed to me." She turned her back on him and ripped her engagement ring off her finger. "You've broken my heart, Elias." She shook her head with disbelief. "It's my fault."

"Daisy, it was never your fault. It's just—" He reached for her and she ripped her arm away.

"Don't you fucking touch me!" Daisy whirled back around and tossed the ring at him. It bounced off his chest and rolled underneath the bed. "It's my fault because I existed, Elias. Maybe I was too possessive over you. Maybe I cared too little. But this whole ordeal has showed me what type of man you really are." She cracked a sneer. "I hope you make her happy." She sauntered into the bathroom and slammed the door behind her.

Elias pressed his ear against the door and listened to hollow echo of her cries. "Daisy, I'm sorry. I don't know what else to say."

"You're abandoning your family to be with another," Daisy cried out inside the bathroom. "I'm pregnant, Elias. Are you going to deny this child?"

"Of course not. I want to be a part of our baby's life."

"Once you walk out that door, I will rebuke all your parental rights. This child deserves more than what you're giving me. What kind of man walks out on his pregnant partner, anyway?"

As much as he hated to admit it, Daisy was right. He turned from the door and retrieved the ring from underneath the bed. He placed it gently on the bedside table, alongside his rose boutonnière. He made an inward promise to be a good father to both children, even if his relationships with their mothers were unstable. He wanted Ava from the first moment he saw her, a desire that scared and liberated him. It was simple and animalistic, an electricity he didn't share with Daisy. Loyalty had betrayed his heart, but passion would keep it beating. He closed the bedroom door behind him and left his life with Daisy behind.

Chapter 27

Elias dashed through the hospital halls, hoping he wasn't too late. He bypassed mothers cradling newborn babies and grandparents dragging tired and uninterested children around the ward. Nurses stepped out of his way, confused by his crumpled wedding suit.

He turned the corner and located Ava's hospital room at the end of the hall. A 'Do Not Disturb' sign hung on the doorknob. He knocked softly and heard muffled voices inside the room. The door opened, and Veronica's exhausted face lit up at the sight of him.

"Elias, what a sight for sore eyes." Her voice was low and hushed. "It's wonderful to see you. Please come in." She welcomed him inside the room, pushing aside the curtain that offered privacy to Ava lying upright in bed.

Elias's heart was pounding if he'd run a marathon. He stood planted on the spot, his eyes firmly fixed on the little bundle pressed against Ava's chest, small and unmoving. The stunning smile she bestowed him reaffirmed his feelings. He loved her. She was the one he wanted to be with.

"Come over and meet your daughter," Ava said softly.

He approached the bed slowly and perched on the edge, welcoming the baby into his arms. She felt so delicate and breakable against his chest. "She's so beautiful. What's her name?"

"Lila."

Elias kissed the baby's soft scalp adorned with bright, copper hair. Her skin was pearl white. "Hello, Lila." He felt the heat of Ava's gaze drawing up and down his body.

"Did you get married today?" she asked. "You're wearing your suit."

He glanced up and found sadness behind her emerald eyes. "No. I've left Daisy for good."

Veronica made a small noise and walked towards the door. "It's best for me to leave. I'll be outside if you need me." She slipped out of the room.

When the door closed behind her, Ava glared wearily at Elias, breathing sharply through her nose. "What did you do, Elias?"

"I chose you and Lila. Isn't that what you wanted?"

"Yes, I do. But what about Daisy?"

"She's not an innocent party," Elias argued. "She betrayed me. I can't forgive what she did. Selling her photos of us to the press was the first mistake she made. I can't trust her anymore."

Ava climbed out of bed and stood opposite him. "So you left her at the altar?"

"No, I told her before the ceremony."

"How dignified of you. How did she take the news?"

"As well as you expect. I didn't make the decision lightly, Ava. I've been thinking of leaving her for months. Abandoning Daisy at the altar wasn't the best thing I've ever done, but it was needed." With his free hand, he cupped her face, stroking her cheek with the pad of his thumb. "I want to be a family. With you and Lila. No more half-assed promises. It's you I want." He leaned forward to kiss her, but Ava rebuffed him.

"I've been waiting for you to say those words for months. But forgive me if I'm not jumping with joy. When I was pregnant, it broke my heart seeing you with Daisy, planning a wedding and an impending arrival. How do you think she feels now that the roles are reversed? She's pregnant with your child. She needs your support more than ever."

"I will give her anything she wants."

"She wants you, Elias. If you're with me, then you can't give her what she truly wants." She turned and sat back down on the bed, pinching the bridge of her nose. "You need to talk to her. You cannot move on with me when there's unfinished business with her. I wouldn't feel right unless it was done. Do you understand? It's important for our children to grow up in a civilised environment."

Elias carefully lowered Lila in her crib and joined Ava on the bed. He kissed her softly, uncaring if she protested. He had missed how she tasted, how she felt under his touch. "I will speak with Daisy. Life's too short to have two women pissed off at you."

Ava smiled, burying her fingers into the depths of his hair. "Stop talking, Elias. I've waited too long for this moment." She bought him in for a passionate kiss.

~ ~ ~

The apartment was quiet when Elias came home on Sunday night. The living room lamp was on as he'd left it, throwing fractured shadows onto the ceiling. There was an eeriness in the air that left goosebumps along his skin. Some of Daisy's belongings that were never fully unpacked were back in boxes, this time stationed around the unit in a uniform manner. Her clothes were hastily thrown into boxes, topped off with shoes, boots, and unbreakable knickknacks. Seeing her things like that offered some comfort and relief that all this was over. Today would've been the start of his honeymoon. A new life that no longer existed.

Elias wandered into the living room to inspect a box full of crockery when the front door opened. Daisy froze at the sight of him, quickly regained her composure and closed the door behind her.

"What are you doing here?" she demanded. "I asked you not to be here while I packed up my stuff."

"I need to talk to you."

She rolled her eyes and dumped her keys on the kitchen bench. "I think I've given you enough chances to talk." She approached a box and rummaged through it. "You've humiliated me. My poor father was forced to explain your absence to the guests. What you've done to me is unforgivable."

"I'm sorry our relationship ended the way it did. But I couldn't keep living the lie. Come on, Daisy. We were fooling each other to think we had a future."

"Did you love her this entire time?"

Elias averted his gaze to the floor. "Yes. I guess I did."

"Why did you propose to me if you felt this way?"

"I don't know why I proposed. I guess I did it to hide my true feelings. I was so conflicted by my emotions for you and her. I thought marrying you would be the right decision. But something happened to you, Daisy. You're a completely different woman."

"Our lives changed the moment you started working with Ava." She sneered at him. "I often wonder if we would be in this situation if you never left Manny Magpie."

"I was getting shit money and the job had no prospects at all. I did it for us."

She laughed. "Really? You were thinking with your other head when you accepted the job at Blue Tail."

He went to stroke her belly when Daisy jumped out of the way. "Why don't you let me touch you?" he asked. "I haven't bonded with the baby at all. Honestly, when you told me you were pregnant, I thought it would change our relationship. It only made things worse."

"There's no baby, Elias." The lack of emotion in her voice sent shivers across his skin.

"What do you mean there's no baby?" Elias probed. "Did you lose it?"

She met his gaze and lifted her shirt to reveal a fake pregnant belly. "You wanted to know why I refused you to touch me. This is the reason. I was never pregnant. Ever." There was nothing on her face to show her remorse, no regret or guilt in her eyes. Dead. Emotionless.

Elias's knees weakened and he pulled out a kitchen stool in time. He covered his face in his hands, grieving for a child that never existed. "You lied me for months! I believed I was going to be a father. You showed me a scan of our baby."

"You can buy fake scans on the Internet," Daisy explained. "You'll be surprised how easy it is."

"Why did you do it?" There was so much Elias wanted to say—no, scream—at her, but he was exhausted of her playing games of deceit. She was toxic, not worthy of any redemption.

"I figured if I was pregnant with your baby, you'll stay with me. You're not the type of man to leave a pregnant woman."

"That's entrapment." Elias got off the stool and peeled the baby scan off the fridge. He ripped it into two pieces, throwing them at her. "You've committed low acts before, but this is the lowest. I came here tonight to discuss our future. Ava wanted our children to grow up in a civilised environment. I can tell her that there's no need for that now."

"It's always about Ava! Always! From day one, she was the topic of conversation," Daisy screamed. "I've had enough hearing her fucking name. She doesn't own you, Elias."

"Neither do you! I've tried my hardest to accommodate you, Daisy. I've ignored the piteous jealousy and the need for control. It's not going to happen anymore. I'm done. We're done."

Daisy shrunk at his outburst and gathered her purse on the kitchen bench. Tears pooled in the corners of her eyes. "I'm sorry it didn't work out between us." She rested a gentle touch on Elias's arm and pressed a ghost-like kiss to his cheek. "I'm sorry your feelings for another woman destroyed this relationship. I'm too tired to fight anymore. Good luck with your new family, Elias. Ava is lucky to have you." Without waiting for a response, she turned, opened the front door and left Elias's life forever.

Chapter 28

The sun's rays felt warm on Ava's cheeks as she read the newspaper at her favourite city café. Lila slept in her pram beside her chair, her little heart-shaped lips pressed together in a pout. Ava never envisioned she could produce something so beautiful, so pure. There were days she would wake up fearing it was all a dream and Lila wouldn't be in her cot. In moments of panic, she would roll over and be comforted by the man sleeping next to her.

She was so proud of Elias. It wasn't easy for him to shed his past life, filled with memories of Daisy. They had a family now. He couldn't afford to be swept up in all the drama. The media interest died down and local newspapers found someone else to write about. Elias kept details of Daisy's fake pregnancy from the press by keeping his mouth shut and his wallet open to journos who found out. It was his one last act of heroics to a woman he didn't have a future with.

Ava couldn't deny she directed a lot of her hate at Daisy for what she did, sabotaging their relationship and causing trouble. The woman clearly needed help. But it was water under the bridge now. It was time to move on.

Elias appeared at the table with two glasses of water and a table number hooked underneath his arm. He sat down, tossing a quick glance at Lila sleeping. "It's wonderful to have a peaceful breakfast without flashing cameras and intrusive public."

"We're yesterday's news, Elias. It's back to normal now."

He flipped open the newspaper and skimmed a few

pages before asking, "Did you hear back about the job with the New York publisher?"

In a bid to flee the suffocating drama in Sydney, Ava applied for jobs in America, believing a change of scenery and a challenging career working for the top book publishers in the country would be therapeutic. "They emailed me last night."

"Come on. Don't leave me hanging. What did they say?"

"I passed my Skype interview," Ava replied. "They want to see me next week for round three. It looks very promising."

Elias leaned over the table and kissed her. "Do it, Ava. This is a job of a lifetime. You can't let this one slip through your fingers. Lila and I will be with you the entire way. We can start a new life in New York."

"What would you do about work? I can't expect you to uproot your life for me."

"I already have." He brushed her hair off her cheek, his touch lingering for a moment. "You were the greatest risk I ever took, Ava. I can take another one."

Ava had never believed in second chances before she met Elias. Now, she was certain they existed. There wasn't much tying her to Australia. Veronica moved into her old mansion and she settled things with Liam before he moved out of state for work. She had her family to look after now.

Ava sat back in her chair and studied the atmospheric CBD around her. Music spilled out of store fronts, cars created an orchestra in the streets, and the golden sun pierced the skyline. She created and built her entire publishing career in this very city, and it almost destroyed her. Still, New York was calling. It was far from the cameras and journalists who knew too much about her personal life. There was always going to be the risk of a person or corporation kicking the hornet's nest, desperate to generate public interest again. But this time she would be far away with the man she loved. "Let's do it," she said. "I'm ready for a change."

Also from **Soul Mate Publishing** and **Kellie Wallace**:

DARKNESS BEFORE DAWN

In June 1940, Germany bombed the Island of Guernsey, bringing World War II to the Channel Islands. With her home in the midst of war, jazz singer Catherine La Mar must adapt to change. Within days, the island is overrun. Resistance cells start to emerge, hindering the German forces. Catherine's life is inevitably changed when childhood friend Thomas Potter is linked as the ringleader to one of the Island's biggest cells.

The people she once knew are no longer who they seem to be. But nothing could prepare her for when she meets Nazi officer Captain Max Engel. Her view on the war forever changes when she is given a chance for love and new beginnings. For once in her mundane life she unveils her true self, as Max teaches her how to truly live. Their love puts a strain on Catherine's family, risking the lives her sisters and friends. As the war intensifies and divides the people on Guernsey, Max and Catherine must decide if their love is really worth risking it all.

Available now on Amazon: <u>DARKNESS BEFORE DAWN</u>

EDGE OF TOMORROW

Twenty years after The Great Global Riots and the collapse of humanity, Alex Locke struggles to save his family, and his home colony of Pena, from starvation. When a letter from the corrupt Govern arrives dictating a game of survival penning local colonies against each other, Alex must trust a childhood friend, and seven others, on a certain death march to win the bounty or lose the only hope left in a war-ravaged world.

Available now on Amazon: **EDGE OF TOMORROW**

EARTHWALKER

Noah is an angel whose job relies on collecting human souls who aren't ready to leave their vessels. To his brothers, Michael and Gabriel, he's just another rookie, earning his arch angel wings. When Noah catches an Earthbound demon in his form stealing a soul, he's sent back to Heaven to plead his case. But no one believes him. Banished from Heaven for a crime he didn't commit, Noah is given one year on Earth to find the demon responsible for his framing. If he fails to do so, he will be dragged to Hell for eternity.

On his first day on Earth, he meets Fern Holliday who helps him get back on his feet. She's reluctant to get close to him, but agrees to help Noah find the demon. By following signs Michael sends him, Noah and Fern travel the world in search of the demon. They grow closer every day until Fern is struck down by a mystery illness. Noah is at loss at what to do as her condition worsens. Before the year is up and he returns to Heaven empty-handed, the demon agrees to be taken back, only if Noah takes Fern's soul to Lucifer. Will he follow the strict rules of Heaven, or succumb to his heart?

Available now on Amazon: **EARTHWALKER**

TO LEAN ON FALLING MEN

Wall Street stockbroker John Forrest thought he had it all. Beautiful wife, booming business, fast lifestyle. But when he wakes up in an open grave in the middle of the desert he begins to question his life. He has no recollection of how he got there or who wants him dead. Found by an Iraqi rebel cell, John is taken hostage and forced to broadcast his plea across Western television.

When Amber Joseph sees her boss's scratchy image on the Internet she vows to bring him home. John arrives in New York and becomes an instant celebrity. The spotlight and the unwanted attention unearth the demons of his past, including his wife's recent suicide. But one question remains. Who left him to die in the middle of the desert, and why?

Available now on Amazon: **TO LEAN ON FALLING MEN**